The Summer of my

Fifteenth Year

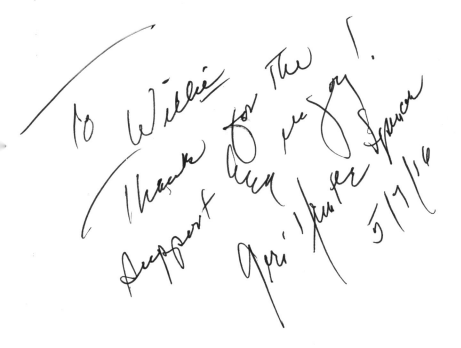

Also by Geri Hunter

Polkadots

The Summer of My Fifteenth year begins like a locomotive train at the station. The engine starting, warming up, "All Aboard!" Then slowly pulling out from the train yard, beginning a wonderful journey through Negro life in the Midwest, when segregation was the standard, yet there were neighbors, Black and white, and especially family, oh yes, family. But the momentum of the train picks up and moves through life itself, the intensity of John Coltrane's saxophone can be heard describing the strife, humor, hurts, sorrow, insanity, love, anger, funky bitterness, and the destructiveness of Black America. At one point, you are afraid to turn the page in fear of what will happen next. Geri Hunter lets you down easy or slows the *trane* and screaming horn to a peaceable close.

Charles Curtis Blackwell, Poet, visual artist, playwright

Geri Hunter has written a painfully poignant tale of lost innocence. She shows a solid family draped in love and guided by strong values. The explosive yet taboo subject that is rarely spoken of leads to a conclusion you're uneasy with and hope you're wrong about, one that will tilt an entire family on its axis, never to be the same again.

Vicki L. Ward, author, publisher of award-winning, **Life Spices from Seasoned Sisters**.

Charlie has always been reckless and cavalier. Upon his return from college, his actions will rock this close knit family to its core. Geri Spencer Hunter's 'The Summer of my Fifteenth Year' is honest and heart wrenching. Readers will not be able to put this one down.

Tonya Manns, Owner, Dynamic Voiceovers

Summer 1937 wasn't going to be a typical summer for Etta and her older sister, Becca because their older brother "Charlie" was returning home from college after two years. Papa has a new car, Becca's going away to college and Etta is turning 15. The threats of thunder storms which plague the mid-west have blown over, the air is filled with childhood fun until one fateful day when innocence is lost and the family, Mama, Papa, Charlie, Becca, and especially Etta, will never be the same. *The Summer of my Fifteenth Year* is a gripping, tightly written novel by Geri Spencer Hunter.

Patricia E. Canterbury, **The Secret of Morton's End**

This novel by Geri Hunter will do what skin care products have promised to do for years…make you younger. The mental imagery conjured by her storytelling will lead the reader to taste, smell, feel and see the youthful times of the author's imagination. Etta's cultural memories of her life are brought to full color reality as she relates her growing-up experiences through the recollection of the Netter family. May the reader prepare to enjoy life again in the literary fountain of youth.

Ron Barnes, author of **Mind Shadows: Tales That Awaken Your Midnight Dreams, and Gold, Silver, Precious, Stones**

The summer of my Fifteenth Year is hard to put down. Hunter's lilting literary voice irresistibly carries the reader wherever she wants the reader to go. This poignant road once taken, like a scene that cannot be un-seen, cannot be un-traveled.'

Naoma Hardy, author

For Ada
Missing you still

Acknowledgements

Special thanks to Dr. David Covin, Blue Nile Press and its staff for making this book possible. Their professionalism, support, and dedication were fantastic. Thanks to my critique group: Jacqueline Turner Banks, Juanita Carr, Pat Canterbury, Shakiri, Ethel Mack Ballard, and Terris McMahan Grimes whose weekly comments and edits were appreciated, most times, and helpful. Thanks to my neat, smart, adult children, nieces and nephews and all their neat, smart adult mates and friends for being neat and smart and always supportive. Last but not least, thanks to Nat Hunter (Hunter), the best thing that ever happened to me!

Library of Congress Cataloguing in Publication Data.

Hunter, Geri Spencer, 1935

1. Black family - 2. Iowa - 3.Great Depression - 4. Female puberty - 5. Sibling conflict - 6 fiction

I. Title

ISBN - 13: 978-0-9844350–5-0

Published by Blue Nile Press

PO Box 188213

Sacramento, CA 95818-8213

Cover Art by Boze

Cover design by Marshall Bailey

Manufactured in the United States of America

Prologue

I ease into my favorite chair and stare at the intimidating little machine on my Formica table. It's tiny and rigid and cold. How can it possibly hold all the memories crowding my mind? They are flipping through my thoughts so fast I can hardly keep up with them. How could that little box allow them to run and play, laugh and cry, fuss, fight, and love, like memories do? But I promised Francesca I would talk into this gadget that's so foreign to me. And I will, Francesca, I will. But first I have to get a handle on my memories. My eighty-six years keep getting in the way of my telling them all.

Like the big white house with its wrap-around front porch where I was born and raised and still live. Where Becca and Charlie and me recklessly pushed each other in the swing that hung from its wood ceiling, back and forth, back and forth, until Mama yelled stop. How we acted like we hadn't heard and pushed even harder. Where we argued over marbles the colors of the rainbow, the size of peas and grapes and baby onions, and Charlie bullying Becca and me for the biggest, and the prettiest, before shooting them in all directions over its worn floor. Becca and I shouting "They're outside the circle" and Charlie ignoring us. Where on hot summer days, we munched on Mama's ginger snap cookies and gulped cold lemonade from shiny tin cups scooping out the uneven ice chunks with our fingers, our bare feet sticky from the dripping liquid.

Like Papa, our Papa, tall and big and light-skinned with fuzzy sandy-colored hair. He was smart and talkative and out going, religious. He seldom drank and never smoked, was a deacon in the church. I remember falling asleep in his lap at Sunday services that seemed to last days instead of hours. I remember him walking us to church on cold winter nights to practice for our Christmas program. I remember him and Mama teaching us our pieces. I remember sitting in the back seat of his old Ford car squeezed between Becca and Charlie fidgeting for more space, Becca fidgeting too and Charlie teasing me. I remember Papa scolding Charlie and Charlie bumping my shoulder hard as pay back.

And Mama. Pretty, pretty Mama, with her coco brown skin, huge brown eyes, thick long kinky hair and ready smile. Her voice was soft and gentle, until Charlie or Becca or I got out of hand, misbehaved, tried to show off. Then it was loud and harsh and threatening, surprising us, always surprising us. I remember how smart Mama was and how talented. She could sew clothes, all kinds of clothes, that looked better then those sold at Sears or J.C. Penny's. I remember Becca and me standing like statues to avoid the pinpricks and Charlie grumbling about wearing homemade clothes. I remember her hair pressing and me trying not to cry when the hot iron got too close and her whispering sorry with tears in her voice. I remember Becca laughing until it was her turn.

And Charleston. I called him Charlie. He was the oldest and the only boy and Papa's favorite. Charlie could do no wrong and whatever Charlie asked for, he usually got. Becca and I were jealous of Charlie. Charlie was cute and looked like Papa. He was pampered, arrogant, egotistical and spoiled. But he was also funny and smart and bossy. When we played hide and seek, he was always the seeker.

Becca and I knew he was cheating, didn't really have his eyes closed, cause he found us too easily. He could draw perfect chalk boxes for hopscotch, and when we played, he never missed a square. On winter days, he pushed our sleds down the small hills hopping on the back for the ride down. He took us to and from school walking so fast Becca and I could hardly keep up. Laughed and teased us for being scared by the weekly radio mystery series, "The Shadow".

And Rebecca. Pretty, loner Rebecca, who I called Becca. She was moody and private and smart, smarter than Charlie, aloof. She didn't always act like a big sister, sometimes treated me like a nobody, like we were enemies instead of siblings. But sometimes, sometimes, she acted like we were best friends. We had tea parties with our dolls, dressed up in Mama's old clothes and shoes, tried to play duets on the piano. We giggled over girly stuff and fussed over nonsense. She helped me with my numbers, my letters, taught me to tie my shoes and read to me for hours.

Memories.

I shake my head to clear my thoughts. I can't possibly tell them all, don't want to tell them all. So I decide to just stick to the ones that had the most impact. I push play on the strange little machine that I don't completely trust yet, and start my telling.

PART 1

ETTA

1

It was summer 1937, early summer, before the sun reached scorching and the rains turned vicious. It was my favorite time of year. School was out and the days were long and lazy and full of discoveries. I spent my time reading, writing poems, practicing the piano or just daydreaming on the shady wrap-around front porch of our house. I loved our house. It was big and white with lots of windows, an upstairs, a basement and that wrap-around front porch. It also had a spacious front lawn, a side yard full of flowers and fruit trees, and a back yard dominated by a huge garden overflowing with beans, tomatoes, onions and radishes, collard greens and mustards, rhubarb, and since we lived in a small Iowa town, corn - rows and rows of sweet, sweet corn.

This day was special. Papa was mowing the yard and trimming the hedges. Mama and my older sister Rebecca and I were busy in the kitchen. My big brother Charlie was coming home.

Charlie had been gone two long years attending Normal Academy, a small colored college in Tennessee. He stayed there during the summers to get the feel of the place, he said, and get to know the people. Why he had to go all that way for college was beyond me, but Charlie was Charlie, always doing things his way. Actually, his name was Charleston, Charleston Epstein Netter, but I called him Charlie, smart Charlie, just because he was, mostly because he hated it and because he was constantly teasing me, calling me bookworm and beanpole, mimicking my movements, mouthing smart remarks and shooing me away like I was some kind of pest. I really wanted to call him smart-ass Charlie, but knew Mama and Papa would never allow that, although I did sometimes under my breath so only he could hear. Yeah, Charlie was a smart-ass, but I was still excited about seeing him. Maybe after two years he had changed.

A gentle breeze was blowing through the open windows of the hot kitchen, swaying the lacy curtains cooling the room. We were cooking Charlie's favorite foods, fried chicken, potato salad, greens and peach cobbler. Well, to be honest, Mama and Becca were doing most of the cooking. Becca had relegated me to clean up, washing pots and pans. Becca was seventeen, had just graduated from high school and would be going off to State college in the fall. She was already acting like some grown-up, trying to boss me around. It really annoyed me, but since I didn't want her to know, on good days I usually did as she ordered. This was a good day.

"Mama, are you going to do all this cooking for my birthday?" I asked, watching her rolling out pie dough. "I'm going to be fifteen." I was only teasing. Mama always celebrated our birthdays with special meals and big fancy cakes.

"Turning fifteen ain't," Becca grumbled.

"Isn't," slipped effortlessly out of Mama's mouth as she continued working the dough and not looking at Becca.

"Isn't," Becca repeated, rolling her eyes, "a big deal, Etta."

"It is to me," I said.

"I forgot, every thing's a big deal to you."

"Shush, Rebecca, birthdays should be a big deal, especially when you're young." Mama lifted the dough off the wooden board and placed it in a wide square glass pan, pressing it down on the bottom and against the sides. Becca opened the jars of still bright yellow peaches Mama had canned last year. She drained them into a big bowl and started adding white sugar, brown sugar, all kinds of spices and several tablespoons of flour while Mama dotted little squares of butter on the bottom of the crust. Even uncooked the cobbler looked delicious.

"Don't I always make your favorite foods?" Mama added, giving me a smile. Mama had the prettiest smile in the world, wide open friendly showing off her even white teeth. Come to think of it, everything about Mama was pretty, her smooth cocoa brown skin, huge dark brown eyes, and thick black hair she kept twisted in a bun or trapped in a hair net. Folks said I looked just like her. Becca, they said, was the spitting image of Papa.

"I was just teasing."

"That's why she's so spoiled," Becca said, making a face at me.

"Look who's talking, all you have to do is whine and pout and Papa gives you any and every thing."

"Does not."

"Does too."

"Will you two stop? You're both spoiled."

"Don't forget about Charleston," Becca said. "He's so spoiled he smells."

Amen to that.

"That's enough, Rebecca."

Becca and I glanced at each other. Mama knew it was true. Charlie was the oldest child and the only boy. Papa loved all of us but Charlie was his favorite. He doted on him. Charlie could do no wrong. When he got in trouble, Papa was there to get him out. When he ignored Mama and Papa's curfew, Papa was usually the one who backed down. When one day out of the blue, he decided he wanted to learn to play the trumpet, Papa bought him one even though Mama disapproved. She thought he was too young; it would interfere with his studies and was probably just a whim. Papa bought it anyway. When he insisted on going south for college, Papa consented although things were tight and there were plenty of good schools closer to home. Papa's excuse, he liked the idea of his son attending a colored school. The truth was Charlie was pampered, arrogant, egotistical, and like Becca said, so spoiled he smelled.

The screen door banged closed and Papa walked into the kitchen. His face was flushed and sweat trickled down its sides and neck damping the front of his shirt. He had on overalls and tie-up shoes. Papa never wore shorts even on the hottest of days and seldom wore overalls. He always had on long pants and shirts and jackets and tie-up shoes.

"Something smells mighty good in here," he said, putting his hands around Mama's skinny waist and kissing her on the cheek.

"Jonas, don't you see I'm cooking." Mama acted annoyed but a smile was on her lips. "What time are you picking up Charleston?" she asked, moving away from the stove and fanning her face with the edge of her apron.

Papa looked at his watch. "I got about an hour and a half if the train's running on schedule, enough time to take a bath and get there."

"Can I go Papa?" I asked.

"Talk to your mother," he said, walking out of the room.

"Can I, Mama?"

"I need you, Etta, to help finish up."

"Why can't Becca do that?"

"Because I've already done more than my share," she said sticking out her tongue.

"You always think you're the only one who helps." I couldn't wait for fall when Becca would be leaving for college.

"Girls, girls," Mama interrupted, "you've both been a big help, but I really do need you, Etta. Besides, it's been a long time since your father and your brother have spent anytime together. They need some alone time."

10

"We haven't seen him either," I said, trying not to sound like I was arguing.

"I know, Baby, but your brother will be here all summer. You'll have plenty of time to catch up. Your daddy will be busy with work."

"I wonder if Charleston will try to find work?" Becca said.

"Why would Charlie want a job?" I asked. "He's just here for the summer."

"He'll need spending money. Besides, it'll give him something to do."

"Jobs are hard to come by these days, Rebecca, even men with families can't find one."

"Not for Charlie, Mama. I bet Mr. Nolan would give him one sweeping up his barbershop. And what about Fryers, Mr. Fry likes him; he'd probably hire him to bag groceries."

Mama sighed. "Not these days, Sweetie."

I looked at Becca and started laughing.

"What's so funny?" she asked.

"Have you forgotten we're talking about Charlie? I can't imagine him wanting a job even in the best of times."

CHARLIE

2

Charleston Epstein Netter was not particularly looking forward to going home. In fact, he was dreading it and trying to come up with some flimsy excuse why he couldn't. Since he wasn't having much success, -none- to be exact, and since his papa had started calling, threatening to cut off his money, he kind of figured he probably had little choice. When a train ticket arrived in his mailbox, he knew it was a done deal. It wasn't that he didn't love his gentle, sweet Mama and smart, talkative Papa. He even loved his sisters, pretty, loner, Rebecca and pesky, irritating, Etta. He truly did. It was just that the Midwest town where he had been born and raised was small and boring and . . . white. He had grown used to that but ever since adolescence, when he wanted boys like him to hang out with, and girls like him to tease, he had hated it. He couldn't wait to grow up and graduate high school and go away to college. He saw college as his way of leaving with Mama and Papa's blessings and support, and his chance to be free. If he could hang on until then, he reasoned, he had it made.

It worked. He got accepted at Normal Academy, a small colored college in Memphis. He wanted to study music. Music was his passion, had been since he talked Papa into buying him a trumpet when he was thirteen. Mama wasn't happy, but Papa stood his ground and let him keep it, like he knew he would. Charleston had discovered early he could always wind Papa around his fingers. Mama had made the same discovery and tried hard to make Papa aware of Charleston's sneaky little antics, was still trying, but Papa refused to listen.   They all knew, Mama, Rebecca, even Etta, that what Charleston wanted, Charleston got.

For two years, two long years, he'd lived there. He loved the city. It was so different from where he had come from, what he had grown up with. It hadn't taken him long to get comfortable with all of it, the people, the language, the style, the rhythm of the place . . . the freedom. He was finally his own boss. He loved that too. No more asking permission, no more strict rules and threatening disciplinary consequences, no more having to tolerate Rebecca's whining or Etta calling him Charlie. And he could still wind Papa around his fingers.

He dug college from the beginning. He was smart and into learning. His Midwest education had been top notch. It had prepared him well. That was one thing he couldn't complain about. His home state put education at the very top of its list. He dug the students too. They came mostly from the south, a few from the north even a sprinkling from the west. They were different and fascinating, but strangely the same. They smoked and drank and dabbled in sex, went to dances and parties, all the things he had wanted to do. He wallowed in it and soaked it up like a sponge. He looked like Papa with light skin and sandy-colored hair and his charming arrogant ways made him popular, especially with the girls. They liked him, called him Charleston and clambered for his attention. He liked them too, got into girls and sex. Girls were familiar. Sex was new. His one sexual experience as a teen had been miserable and almost got him in trouble. It scared him, forced him to leave sex alone, back off and put it aside. Now that he was older, more mature, and the girls more willing, he got into it again, got reacquainted and loved that too.

He kept busy with studies, girls, and music, especially music. He had talent. Time passed and his first year was over, but he wasn't ready to go home back to the boring small town where nothing much happened and folks only talked about each other. He made up excuses,

13

all kinds of excuses, and stayed, playing his trumpet, hanging out with his musical buddies and the girls. But, his excuses were growing thin and Papa was beginning to see thru his nonsense, demanding his return.

He admitted, sometimes, he missed home and the more he thought about going, the more he wanted to go. He missed Mama's cooking; Papa's catering to his every whim, even pretty, sullen Rebecca and skinny bookworm Etta. It would be nice to lounge on the wrap around front porch, pick apples off the trees and fresh tomatoes out of the garden. It would be nice to hear Mama fussing around in the kitchen, smell chicken frying and cakes baking, eat formally at the table in the dining room. He knew it wouldn't last, knew within a week or less, he'd be bored and on edge, anxious to return to college.

Although he wrote occasionally, it was Mama and Papa's frequent letters that kept him informed. He knew Papa had a new car but didn't know what kind. Papa hadn't said. Only that he bought a car, like that was enough. He knew Rebecca had graduated from high school and would be going to State College in the fall. He knew Etta was growing up. He vaguely wondered if her body had started developing, or was still kid stick skinny? He knew their church had been selected to host the big yearly conference all the churches competed for each summer. And he knew, without them telling him, the town had not changed. He was in no hurry to return.

But Papa had finally put his foot down and even though he could still wind Papa around his fingers, he knew his limits. So, after living in the south for two long years, Charleston Epstein Netter said his temporary good-byes, packed his bags and his trumpet, boarded the Zephyr going north, and headed home, wondering how he was going to survive what he knew was going to be a very boring summer.

14

ETTA

3

We were sitting on the front porch, just the three of us. Mama had given Becca and me a break from kitchen duty to chitchat with Charlie. Becca and I were swaying gently in the swing suspended from the wooden ceiling. Charlie was relaxing in the wicker armchair, his long legs stretched out in front of him and crossed at the ankles, his feet resting on the porch's wide railing.

Charlie seemed different. He had filled out a little and was slightly taller and his hair had gotten lighter looking more like Papa's. In looks, he was still Charlie, but he was different too, in other ways, ways I couldn't quite put my finger on. Maybe because he was grown, wasn't a kid any more?

"Etta," he said, grinning. "You've certainly changed."

"Charlie, you've just gotten here, how do you know I've changed?" He actually called me Etta. I couldn't remember the last time he had called me by my name. It sounded good and I was glad to see him.

"Etta, Etta, Etta," he said, still grinning, "looking at you definitely tells me beanpole is no longer appropriate. You aren't skinny anymore, not all arms and legs."

I laughed and had to admit he was right. At thirteen I was all arms and legs. "My body has changed, but not my mind. I'm still obnoxious," I said, trying to ignore his gaze. He was staring at my face but I could feel his eyes all over my body.

"Yeah, but just look at you," he said.

Charlie was making me uncomfortable. Had I changed that much? I mean I had gotten taller, my body had filled out in certain

15

places and those awful periods had started, but like Mama told me, they were natural changes, just a part of becoming a woman. So, what was Charlie's problem? "What about Becca?" I asked.

"Rebecca is pretty as ever," he said, dismissing her and continuing to stare at me.

I looked at Becca. She was grinning like some Cheshire cat. I knew Becca thought she was cute. "How was the ride home?" I asked, wanting to move his talk away from me.

"Fantastic. The Zephyr is truly a first class train. It's the only way to travel; the absolute best way to see the countryside."

"You're such a snob, Charleston," Becca said, laughing and shaking her head. Becca was in a good mood for a change.

"Preferring the finer things in life doesn't make me a snob, right Etta?"

"I agree with Becca. You are a snob."

"Call me what you will. I refuse to apologize for enjoying elegance. Speaking of which, the Packard is really something. It's classy and luxurious. I didn't know Papa had that kind of class."

"Surprise, surprise, you are not the only one with taste. "

"Where did he get the money?"

"Ask him."

"Maybe I will.

"I dare you."

"God, I can't wait to get behind the wheel," he said, ignoring me.

"You know how to drive?" I tried not to sound too impressed.

"A little, but Papa said he'd teach me."

Becca and I looked at each other.

"Smart Charlie getting his way again," I said, unable to resist.

"Dinner's ready," Mama called.

16

We always dressed for dinner. Mama wore a white cotton blouse with three quarter length sleeves, a full bright blue linen skirt with a wide red belt. Her long pressed hair was brushed in waves and coiled in a thick roll in the back that swayed softly. A faint shade of red stained her lips and cheeks. Becca and I had on colorful sleeveless sundresses and sandals. Papa was Papa. Linen pants, cotton shirt, lightweight Jacket and tie-up shoes. Charlie still had on his traveling clothes, seersucker suit, striped cotton sport shirt open at the collar and saddle shoes.

The one thing about Charlie that hadn't changed was his appetite. He was eating like he hadn't had a meal in months.

"Mama, this is delicious," he said stuffing his mouth. "I swear I haven't had such a good meal since I left home." He swallowed and gave her an open smile. He looked like Papa but had Mama's smile.

"Quit teasing, Son," Mama said, sounding pleased.

"I'm serious."

Everything was delicious. The chicken's skin was crisp, the meat moist and juicy. The spicy greens were tender and the potato salad creamy. The hot water cornbread was golden brown and crunchy. I couldn't wait for the cobbler.

Unlike Charlie, Papa was so busy beaming he was hardly eating. "Tell us about college, Son," he said, dabbing his lips with the big square cloth napkin and placing it beside his plate.

Charlie took a sip of ice tea. "What do you want to know, Papa?"

"Well, you've been away from home a long while and your letters were few and far between. Catch us up on what's been happening in your life, how you've been doing."

"I'm healthy."

"We see that."

"What Papa really wants to know is what you've been up to and are you learning anything," Becca said, picking the crispy skin off a chicken leg and slipping it between her lips.

"Yeah, Charlie, do you have a girlfriend, do you smoke, drink, who do you hang out with, you know, stuff like that," I added and saw a frown forming on his forehead.

"College is great," he said, ignoring Becca and me. "I'm doing quite well as you know since you've seen my grades. I've decided to major in music."

"Are you serious, Son?" Papa asked.

Charlie nodded. "I'm taking advance classes with emphasis on the trumpet. I even play in a small band."

"I didn't send you all the way south to learn how to play a trumpet," Papa said, staring at him. "You already know that. You need to be learning a profession."

"Music is a profession, Papa."

"You know what I mean. I'm talking engineering or doctoring or something you can count on in hard times."

"Your father's right, Charleston," Mama said. "Studying music seems like such a luxury in these hard times."

"Times aren't always going to be hard, Mama."

"But music?" Papa said, shaking his head.

"Why are you so surprised? You know music is my first love."

"I know, Son, but you're bright. You need to think of your future, give it more thought."

"I have Papa."

That takes care of that I thought.

"Jonas," Mama said, "we've got all summer to discuss Charleston's education. Right now, let's just enjoy his homecoming."

Papa sighed. "Do you have a girlfriend," he asked, surprising us. "Do you drink or smoke?"

Charlie laughed the frown increasing on his forehead. "Girls, yes, but no girlfriend and I do smoke and drink, a little."

"What's a little, Son?" We couldn't believe Papa was being so persistent.

"My drinking is mostly social, Papa, at a party or when I'm out with friends and I smoke probably less than five cigarettes a day." There was annoyance in Charlie's voice. I guess he didn't like having to be accountable for a change.

"Can he smoke and drink in our house, Papa?" Becca asked, playing with her food. Becca always played with her food and got by with leaving half of it on her plate.

Papa looked at Charlie. Papa seldom drank and didn't smoke. "He's a man," he said, "free to do as he likes."

But it's our house I wanted to say. I didn't. I really didn't care. It was the fact that Papa was taking his beloved Charleston's side again. Just once, I wanted him to say no to Charlie.

Mama served the cobbler with homemade ice cream. It was more than delicious. I ate mine slowly savoring every spoonful. Becca was savoring hers too. Papa was steadily eating and asking Charlie if he wanted to go with him to his office. Charlie's cobbler was gone. He was asking for more and saying yes to Papa although it didn't sound like he meant it. Mama wasn't having any desert. She wasn't much on sweets. She started clearing away the dishes and taking them to the kitchen.

"Do you want help?" I asked, crossing my fingers and hoping she'd say no.

"You've done enough, Etta, enjoy your brother."

"I'll give your mother a hand." We couldn't believe those words had come out of Papa's mouth. "I still know how to bust suds," he said, picking up glasses and silverware and following Mama into the kitchen.

I caught Charlie staring at me, again, a grin on his full lips. What was going through his mind?

"Charleston, why do you keep looking at Etta?" Becca asked, stealing the words out of my mouth.

I heard annoyance in her voice. Had Charlie once looked at her the same way? Then I remembered the gossip, the whispering rumors about Charlie and touching and a teenage girl. I was eleven maybe twelve, didn't understand all of what they were saying or what it meant and didn't get the whole story. I just remembered the arguing, the crying, the denials and the threats. Was Becca remembering too? Charlie laughed and interrupted my memories.

"Sorry, Etta, but I can't get over how you've changed."

"Oh come off of it Charlie. I haven't changed that much. You were just too busy teasing to notice."

"Maybe," he said, not sounding totally convinced.

"It doesn't matter," Becca said, not hiding her annoyance, "she's still just Etta so stop gawking."

"Yeah," I said, "I'm still just Etta."

CHARLIE

4

Charlie laughed, again, but kept his thoughts to himself. He knew she wasn't still just Etta. Still just Etta had been skinny, all arms and legs, an awkward boring kid. This Etta was cute bordering on pretty. Her body seemed to be slowly filling out in all the right places on the verge of becoming a woman and she seemed to be developing those small sensual feminine gestures that she wasn't yet aware of. She fascinated him. He had been dreading coming home not sure how much had really changed. Now he was glad he had. Mama and Papa hadn't aged much and Rebecca had grown into a gorgeous young lady like he had predicted. Etta was the surprise. Two years had turned her into almost a stranger, someone he was interested in really getting to know. He had certainly had his share of girls. They seemed to like musicians and were always hanging around the small crowded joints where he played. They were cute, pretty girls but no longer seemed fresh and innocent . . . like her. He continued looking at her. His summer might not be as boring as he'd thought. He shook his head trying to keep that thought from simmering in his mind and switched his attention to Rebecca.

"Rebecca, welcome to the club."

"What in the world are you talking about, Charleston?"

"You know the club. You've graduated from high school, that makes you a member of the thank God that's over I'm finally free club," he said, laughing.

"Just because I graduated does not make me free," she said, not laughing, not even smiling. "Besides, that sounds like something you made up."

"I did," he admitted. She was as sullen as he remembered. *Relax, he wanted to tell her, nothing's that serious.* "You don't appreciate my humor?"

"Not particularly."

"Becca has no sense of humor," Etta said.

"It wasn't funny, okay."

"Sorry," Charlie said, "are you excited about college?"

"Of course."

"Why don't you sound like it?"

"What is this, Charleston, pick on Rebecca hour?"

"Are you always like this?" he asked and saw Etta vigorously nodding her head.

"Like what? You haven't even been home a whole day and you're already trying to judge somebody. You haven't changed."

"I'm not judging, Rebecca, I'm trying to reconnect with you and Etta get to know you again. We haven't seen each other in two years."

"You're our brother, Charleston, how much getting to know us do you need? Like I said Etta is still Etta and I'm still me."

"Be honest, Becca, we have changed so has Charlie."

"That's what I've been trying to say, Etta."

"But not as much as you seem to think. Becca's right, she's still just her and I'm still just me."

"If you say so, but I'm curious how you think I've changed."

"I'm not sure yet. You just got home."

"I'm stuck here all summer. Is that long enough?"

Etta laughed. "I'll let you know when it's over, okay?"

"Okay," he said, laughing too. *Yeah, getting to know Etta just might make for an interesting summer.*

ETTA

5

Charlie had been gone so long his presence shifted our household routine throwing off its rhythm. He wasn't used to eating on a regular schedule, going to church on Sundays, smoking only outside or on the porch or going to bed at ten o'clock. He probably wanted to stay out all night playing his trumpet, but nothing much was happening in our town, so he was stuck at home. I had to give it to Charlie, though. He really could play the trumpet. He made it seem easy and natural each note flowing effortlessly into the next and the next, making me want to give in to its beauty. I wanted to play the piano like Charlie played the trumpet.

Charlie could still play Papa too. He talked him into having a drink or two in the evenings and drew him into heated discussions. They argued about the depression, the economy, how the President was handling the situation and where the country was headed. Papa was in seventh heaven. He loved a good argument, loved that his son was smart and sophisticated and seemed passionate about things that mattered. He was excited about spending his days with him.

Papa sold insurance and had clients not only in our town, but also in numerous small towns around the county. He owned his own business and was the only colored man who had a small office downtown on Main Street. Everybody in town knew him. He was talkative, outgoing and friendly, treated everybody the same. He was a deacon in the Cumberland Presbyterian Church, the colored Presbyterians, and was active in the town's affairs, at least as active as those in charge allowed. He was always talking about running for mayor but everybody including him knew it was just talk. Our town of mostly white folks was fairly friendly and receptive but no way ready for a colored mayor. The thing is, Papa would have been a great mayor. Papa was smart. He had a high school diploma and a certificate in finance from Calamine College. He bragged about how he predicted the depression and how nobody believed him. How he believed in himself and started saving his money, stashing it away in his office safe. He still laughed about how dumbfounded they all were after the fact. Poor Papa, he would have made a great mayor and he continued saying stuff like, "When I'm mayor," or, "Just wait till I'm mayor," knowing it was just talk.

Papa was a great salesman though. Even during these hard times people still managed to scrap up money for their weekly policy payments, afraid if something happened to them their families would be left wanting. He spent his days driving from town to town, practically lived in his car. That's why he had invested some of his money in the Packard, for its reliability and comfort, not necessarily for its prestige. Mama worried a lot when he was on the road. She was always fretting about him getting caught in summer's crazy storms or in winter blizzards when the roads were icy slick and covered with snow. Many nights the weather did stop him from coming home, forcing him to sleep over at a client's house. There were no hotels and the few boarding houses that were available did not welcome Coloreds.

While Papa was driving up and down the highways, Mama was home. Mama was a housewife. I thought housewife was such a dumb way to describe Mama. Mama was married to Papa not to our house.

"Don't be silly, Etta," Becca said, "housewife means Mama stays at home doesn't have to work"

"What do you call what she does all day?"

24

"You know what I mean," she said, rolling her eyes. "Unlike some of her friends, Mama doesn't work in white women's houses just stays at home and works in ours."

"I know that, Becca. It still sounds dumb."

Mama was smart too, and talented. She could sew dresses and skirts and blouses even pants and shirts so good they looked better than the ones in the Sears catalogue or from J.C. Penny's. She made most of our clothes, and to bring in extra money, she sewed for her friends and the rich white women who lived on Main Street.

Papa and Mama were also religious. Every Sunday we went to the Cumberland Presbyterian Church. It used to be a white Methodist church before they moved uptown and the colored Presbyterians bought it. It was a big white stately church with wide steps, stained glass windows and a grand steeple. Papa was a deacon and Mama sang in the choir. Her voice was high and clear sounded like some proud boastful bird singing God's praises.

Mama loved Sunday. It was her favorite day of the week. On Sunday she had Papa all to herself. They'd go for walks, listen to a sermon or some classical concert on the radio or just sit quietly reading or talking to each other. Occasionally, Papa took us to Queenie's, a little restaurant owned by a colored woman who had wandered into our small town one hot summer's day and never left. She cooked in white people's kitchens until, it was whispered, she got help from a well-known citizen to open her own. The town folks loved it. The food was good and different and the prices reasonable. The depression was plaguing her too, since only people with money could afford to eat out. Her business was hanging on by a slender thread, but Papa being Papa still managed to take us there off and on.

I stop my words. Even after all these years, I can still see Mama and Papa and Charlie and Becca and me dressed in our Sunday best eating at Queenie's. I can almost taste her juicy pork roast; creamy scalloped potatoes and buttery fried sweet corn, still making my mouth water. I sigh out loud, dab at the tears trickling down my cheeks and continue my telling.

CHARLIE

6

Charlie couldn't get used to being home. He was bored and restless and being a night owl, stayed up long after everybody else had gone to bed, craving a cigarette and quietly practicing his trumpet. He wished there was some place to go, some place where he could drink and smoke, flirt with the girls and listen to music, even play a few notes. God, he missed that. He thought about trying to hook up with his old high school buddies but quickly dismissed the thought. They'd never had the same taste and he doubted that had changed. He thought of going to the city but didn't have a car, which wasn't a problem. He knew Papa would let him use his. Not knowing how to drive was the big deal. He could've kicked himself. Several of his classmates had offered to teach him, but after one or two lessons, he really wasn't interested. He was too busy learning to play his trumpet. Now, he regretted it. Being able to drive was the obvious solution. Papa had already volunteered to teach him. He figured the quickest way to do that was to spend his days with him. When Papa had mentioned it, he hadn't been too enthused, had just agreed not to hurt his feelings. He rapidly changed his mind and grudgingly fell into Papa's routine.

It wasn't easy. Papa got up early, and after his personal rituals of bathing, shaving and dressing, he fixed his own breakfast. He seemed to get pleasure out of that simple task and always cooked the same things: two slices of toast, two boiled eggs and a thick slice of ham and several cups of strong coffee with sugar and cream. He believed a hardy breakfast was the best way to start the day and enjoyed drinking his coffee and reading his newspaper. It was usually his only quiet time. He was pleased Charleston was coming along and offered to make him breakfast too. But Charlie wasn't much on breakfast. He didn't think it quite normal to eat that early. It was hard enough getting up and dressed by the time Papa was ready to leave and he much preferred sleep to food.

Mama was pleased too. She seemed to think Charleston could protect Papa from she wasn't sure what, but with him along, she didn't seem to worry as much. He didn't remember Mama being such a worrier. Growing up, Charleston thought of her as stable, steady as a rock, able to handle anything and tough, at least on him. She never let him get away with stuff like Papa, probably still wouldn't. Maybe she worried about Papa now because he was getting older and on the road so much. Maybe she was afraid he'd nod off at the wheel or run off the road or into another car. He didn't quite know how he could protect Papa, but if that made her worry less, that was okay with him.

After riding around with Papa for a few days, Charlie began to understand Mama's concern. Papa wasn't the best driver. He was slow and methodical and not always attentive. He wasn't the best teacher either. He insisted Charleston get to know the car and read the drivers manual before getting behind the wheel.

"I can do both at the same time, Papa."

"That'll be too confusing, Son."

Papa's response surprised him. Where was the Papa he was used to, the one he could wrap around his finger? This Papa was new to him. But Papa was serious about his car and his driving. Maybe that explained it. So, he didn't argue just sat in the passenger seat, day after day, listening to Papa going on and on about the floor shifter, the eight-cylinder engine, its 120-horsepower and eighty-five mile an hour top speed. Charlie couldn't have cared less. All he wanted was to learn how to drive so he could be mobile. But having no choice, he endured and was impressed by Papa's knowledge. Papa knew all there was to know about his car and treated it with respect.

He seldom drove at the speed limit, no less over it, never allowed smoking and kept it maintained and in mint condition.

"If you treat your car with respect, it'll never let you down. Remember that, son."

"Yes, Papa."

Papa was also knowledgeable about insurance. Charlie though it was going to be dull and boring listening to him trying to sell insurance policies all day. Instead, he was fascinated. Papa had a real knack for selling and could charm folks into almost anything. He'd never thought of Papa as a professional, smart and well spoken yes, but in his eyes not quite up there with the white men on Main Street. He was beginning to change his mind, beginning to get a new perspective on Papa. He never thought of his home state as pretty, either, but riding though all the quaint little towns day after day, he was beginning to get a different perspective on that too.

ETTA

7

The town we lived in was small, almost rural, surrounded by farms and you could walk to most places you needed to go. Charlie complained there was nothing to do and everybody knew everybody else's business. And of course, Becca complained about everything. Not only that it was small, but it was also too hot, too cold, rained too much in summers and snowed too much in winters. That was true; all of it, but it was also neat and safe, fastidiously clean and mostly white. It had its class people, of course, like the doctors, the lawyers, the storekeepers and the bankers, the preachers. It had two small hospitals, several banks, a Kresges's Five and Dime, one movie house, one elegant hotel for whites only, although there were no signs stating that, a daily newspaper, a library, a charming little train station and a tacky Greyhound bus stop inside Woolworth's drug store. Except for the train station, most of the businesses were up town on Main Street.

The biggest city in the state was fifty miles away. It had streetcars, a huge fancy train station, department stores, movie houses and museums and banks and amusement parks, music stores that carried a big selection of instruments and sheet music and yardage shops with all kinds of fabrics and patterns. It also had numerous hotels and boarding houses and more colored people. The coloreds even had their own neighborhoods, boarding houses, and one gorgeous hotel.

Unlike the city, there weren't a lot of colored people in our town, so there was no official colored section. We were scattered all over, but we knew our place. Certain areas were strictly for whites, like uptown on Main Street.

We lived between two white families. On one side lived the Goddard's. They had a bunch of kids and a narrow attitude. They tried very hard to be stuck-up, at least the papa did. The mama was fairly friendly and the kids played with us. On the other side lived the Bakkes who also had a houseful of kids and very different attitudes. They were Catholics, went to church everyday for a short time, instead of all day, and only on Sundays, like us. And their kids went to catholic school.

Mavis was my age, pale and kind of chubby with straight wispy blonde hair that she was always playing with, and gray-green eyes. She was so different from me. I was tall and skinny with coco-brown skin and kinky hair that Mama had to hot comb to get straight and it still didn't look like hers. I envied Mavis.

Mavis was my friend but Angela was my best friend. We studied at the library, went to the movies, shared ice cream sodas at the lunch counter at the five and dime, borrowed each others' books and struggled to write poems in the swing on the wraparound porch. Angela lived across town. Her papa worked at the packinghouse and her mama worked for rich white women. Angela went with her sometimes, especially on holidays. She hated it. You're lucky your mama doesn't work in white women's houses, she was always saying, making me glad Mama was a housewife.

Angela's family was Presbyterian, too. We met at church when we were nine or ten. We were in the same grade but at different schools until we got to junior high. Our town had only one junior and one senior high school. Both were not far from her house. Mama often let me go home with her, even spend nights. Angela's mama was quiet and calm, pretty, like her. Nothing seemed to upset her. She never raised her voice like Mama. Her papa did, though. There were times he was so loud he scared me. He seemed to scare Angela and her brothers and sisters, too. I think he even scared her mama but she tried to act as if he didn't.

Maybe that was why Angela was quiet, almost shy, didn't do a lot of talking. Becca didn't like her much, said she wasn't friendly - as if she had room to talk. I think Angela felt the same about her. She liked Charlie though, thought he was cute, was constantly asking about him. When she came to our house, she seemed to forget her shyness, spent most of the time trying to talk to him, laughing at his stupid jokes or listening to him struggling to play the trumpet. Charlie acted like she was a pest, didn't give her much attention, treated her like he treated me, with teasing and name-calling. Angela was into music. She seemed to have a natural talent for playing the piano. She just put her hands on the keys and the music flowed. I think Charlie was jealous. He had talent, too, but had to work at it. He probably wished he could play the trumpet as easily as she played the piano. Somehow I suspected she knew that. Mama always said she seemed older than her age.

"What does that mean, Mama?"

"That's just an expression grown-ups use for children who seem to have advanced wisdom."

"Am I older than my age?"

Mama laughed and gave me a hug. "Etta, you are right on target."

I laughed, too, not exactly sure what that meant.

Now, after all those years, Charlie was still whining about our town. He was right, it hadn't changed but he knew that before he got here. I really wanted him to shut up. Papa was the one who insisted he come home. Besides, I liked our town. I liked you could walk to school, to church, to Main Street. I liked that my friend Mavis lived right next door and I could walk to my best friend Angela's house.

I liked I could spend hours at the library and stop for an ice cream soda at Kresges's Five and Dime. I liked our charming little train station, even kind of liked our tacky old bus stop in Woolworth's drug store.

I liked that Angela used to have a crush on Charlie and he treated her like a pest. Did she still? Since he was home for the summer, I thought about asking her. Angela had changed too, was going through all those natural womanly changes like me. How would Charlie treat her now? Would he stare at her like he stared at me? Would she like his attention or be uncomfortable and embarrassed feeling his eyes all over her body?

I liked that Mama was right, that Angela really was an old soul, maybe because she was responsible for her younger siblings and didn't have time for kid things. She could still play the piano better then anybody I knew, but hearing Charlie play the trumpet, now, I thought his talent had caught up with hers, maybe even surpassed it.

So, as much as I hated to admit it, I had to agree with Charlie. Our town was little and boring and mostly white, but it was also Mama and Papa and Becca and me and Mavis and Angela and church and Sundays and occasionally eating at Ms. Queenie's.

It was home!

ETTA

8

Charlie had been working with Papa for a while, driving up and down the highways selling insurance usually from dawn to dusk. This Saturday they were home early for a change. The evening was hot, only a slight breeze trickling through the opened windows making it halfway bearable. We were eating dinner in the dining room. As long as I could remember, dinner was always served in the dining room with starched tablecloths and napkins, Mama's good china, glasses, and silverware. Mama was very strict about eating etiquette. Only breakfast and lunch were eaten informally at the big round wooden table in the kitchen. Even when Papa was gone, Mama, Charlie, Becca, and I still ate formally in the dining room. Using good things just for special occasions or for special folks was a waste, Mama fussed. "Besides, who's more special than my family?"

Papa sat at the head of the table. There was no mistaking who was the man of the house. Mama sat at the end. There were times she sat on the side with Charlie, but not that night. Becca and I sat on the opposite side. We were dressed up as usual.

Papa wiped his mouth and glanced around the table. He cleared his throat to get our attention. "All of you will be pleased to know Charleston is doing quite well with his driving," he said, like he thought we would be as pleased as him.

Becca and I said nothing, just stole a quick look at each other.

Mama smiled at Charlie. "Do you hear that girls?"

"Are you actually driving?" I asked, curious but not wanting to hear him brag.

"Finally".

"Where?"

"Yesterday I drove to Tullston and I drove back from Ardenia today, and Papa didn't have to correct me at all, right Papa?" Tullston and Ardenia were the next towns over, about ten, fifteen miles down the highway.

Papa nodded. "He did very well. I'm beginning to feel much safer when he's behind the wheel."

"Wow, Charlie's driving," I said impressed in spite of myself.

"It's no big deal. In fact it's rather easy." He was grinning and his voice was full of confidence.

"Yeah, tell me that after you take the test," I said, making a face at him.

He shrugged. "Like I said, it's no big deal."

"When are you going to teach me, Papa?" Becca piped up, fiddling with her food, pushing it around and around on her plate with her fork.

"Maybe when you get older, Rebecca, I'll consider it."

"But I'm seventeen, Papa, already two years older than I need to be," she whined, "and I'll be going away to college soon."

"In case you haven't noticed, Sis, you're a girl," Charlie said. "Girls don't drive."

"Says who?"

"It's the law," he said.

"Is that true, Papa?" I asked suddenly mad at Charlie and feeling sorry for Becca. Why couldn't Becca drive? She was smarter than Charlie.

"Your brother's teasing. There is no such law."

"I really thought there was," Charlie insisted, "I don't see women driving."

"Why don't you drive, Mama?" I asked. If Mama could drive, we wouldn't have to wait around for Papa all the time.

Mama shook her head. "I have no interest in trying to steer a car, Etta. It's too much like work and I have enough of that to do already. That's probably why you don't see women driving, Charleston, most women agree."

"It looks more like fun to me," I said. "Is it fun Charlie?"

"It's beyond fun."

"When Papa?" Becca repeated.

"Yeah, Papa, when?" I asked, thinking the sooner Becca learned the sooner it would be my turn. "Can't you teach Becca too while you're teaching Charlie?"

"One student at a time is quite enough and Rebecca's turn will come."

"Why does Charleston get to learn and not me?" Becca was still whining and I could hear tears in her voice.

"Rebecca, you heard your father. Your turn will come," Mama said, reaching across the table and patting her hand.

"But it's not fair," Becca insisted.

"Enough is enough Rebecca." Papa's voice was firm. "We'll talk about this at another time."

Becca shut up. Her head was down and I could tell she was on the verge of crying. I slipped my hand under the table and squeezed her thin leg wanting her to know I was on her side. She moved away.

Dinner was ruined. Mama asked Papa about his day and they tried to include all of us but Becca was still whimpering, I didn't have anything to say and if Charlie did, he shut up for a change. Maybe he was feeling guilty. Becca had told the truth. It wasn't fair. Maybe that's why he hadn't said anything, but knowing Charlie, I doubted it.

It was never much fun being around Becca, but after her little spat with Papa, it wasn't any fun at all. She moped around the house with a pout on her pretty face making it not so pretty and grumbled about everything. I really, really tried to be sympathetic, put myself in her place, but after a week, her whining and complaining were getting on my nerves.

"I wish you'd get over it, Becca," I told her. We were cleaning up the kitchen and she was doing what had become her tiresome routine. "You know Papa's not going to change his mind."

"But, it's not fair," she yelled, slamming a pan down on the counter.

"Will you stop, or do you want Mama coming in here?"

"I don't care, let her," she yelled again.

"Why are you mad at Mama?"

"Mama could have taken my side," she said, "but she never stands up to Papa. She goes along with whatever he says."

"No she doesn't." I tiptoed to the kitchen door and peeked around the edge, relieved Mama was nowhere in sight. I was tired of how Becca was acting but didn't want her to get a whippin.

"She does too. She never takes my side. I'll be glad when I leave."

"You don't mean that."

"I do mean it. Why do you think Charleston stayed gone so long?"

"Charlie just wanted to get used to living in the south. You know Charlie."

"Oh Etta," she said and I heard the disgust in her voice. "You are such a baby. Charleston didn't come home because he liked not being under Papa and Mama's rules. He liked being his own boss doing as he pleased."

"How do you know?"

"Ask him."

"I don't believe much of what he says anymore."

"I'll just be glad when I leave."

I stared at Becca. "Won't you miss us?"

"No," she said simply.

I don't know why that surprised me or why I felt tears gathering in the corners of my eyes.

CHARLIE

9

Charlie hated to admit it, but Rebecca had a point. She was old enough to drive and Papa probably could be teaching her too, at least have her learning the car parts and reading the driver's manual. But her persistence and complaining were trying his patience, making it real hard for him to feel sorry for her. Besides, he rationalized; if she knew the hell Papa put him through she wouldn't be in such a hurry.

And it was hell. Papa finally let him behind the wheel after he knew the car from head to toe and had practically memorized the manual. He was nervous and scared but tried not to show it. He found out immediately it wasn't easy. He already knew that from reading the manual, but actually doing it was even more complicated and scary and he wasn't sure he could.

"Take your time, Son," Papa said, straightening up in the passenger seat. They were parked on one of Papa's way stations as he called them, a skinny two lane deserted road that ran parallel to the main highway. Papa had numerous way stations where he stopped to eat lunch, take a quick nap or take a break from driving.

Charlie wriggled in the seat trying to get comfortable. He took a deep breath, rubbed his hands on his pant legs and put one hand on each side of the steering wheel, gripping it so tight his knuckles hurt.

"Relax," Papa chuckled, "it's not going anywhere until you start the engine."

Papa, I'm not stupid, he wanted to tell him. Instead, he took another deep breath, wriggled in his seat, again, took his right hand off the wheel, and put the key in the ignition.

"Remember you have to press the clutch all the way down, press lightly on the gas pedal then turn the key."

Charlie struggled to follow Papa's instruction. He turned the key and heard the soft purring of the engine.

"Purrs just like a cat," Papa said, grinning.

The car jerked and bounced and stopped dead.

Papa saw the surprised look on Charlie's face and tried not to laugh. "It's a real delicate balance, Son. You've got to learn to coordinate all the movements, get them in sync."

"Another foot would help," Charlie grumbled.

"Well, since you only have two, they'll have to do. Try it again."

Charlie tried it again and again and again. He understood what Papa was saying but he couldn't do it. He couldn't press down on the gas pedal, engage the clutch and keep the car straight all at the same time. Everything felt foreign and out of control. Why had he thought he could learn to drive in one session. It had seemed so easy from the passenger's side. After numerous attempts, he managed to keep the engine running long enough to maneuver the car a little ways down the road.

"Don't forget to steer it."

I know, he almost yelled as he struggled to keep the car on the narrow road.

"Now you know why I chose this spot," Papa said, laughing. "There's seldom any traffic so you can't run into another vehicle just off the road. Put more pressure on the gas pedal, Son, get it up to speed so you can shift into the next gear," Papa instructed.

That wasn't easy either. He tried not to panic. Papa calmly put his hand on the wheel steadying the car, keeping it straight as Charlie pressed on the gas pedal getting up enough speed to shift.

"Now all you have to do is keep it straight," Papa said.

Charlie was surprised by Papa's calmness. If he was afraid or apprehensive, he never showed it, except every now and then when he reminded him to press on the gas, shift, and keep the car on the right side of the road.

Charlie thought he'd never get it, never get the hang of keeping the engine running, no less the shifting, the stalling, restarting, and the hills. He would never learn that delicate balance and coordination required keeping everything in sync. But he didn't give up. He kept trying through failure after failure and frustration after frustration until, slowly but surely, he did. Then it was almost easy and almost fun.

Papa started letting him drive for longer distances and longer periods of time. If it were a short trip, he let him do all the driving and began to relax while he was behind the wheel, even nodded off sometimes. Charlie knew then he had earned his confidence.

He was in a hurry to take the driving test so he could be free of Papa, but Papa kept insisting he wasn't ready.

"Slow down, Charleston, you need more time handling the car, more time on the road and more experience with traffic. You also need to get familiar with the rules so you can pass the test first time around."

"Okay, Papa."

"Don't be in such a rush. You'll get there."

So he took his time, got to know the roads and the rules, and got comfortable with the traffic. He got to really know the car and started developing the coordination needed to keep its delicate balance

41

in sync. Papa was right. He passed the test easily, got his license, and was legally able to drive.

The first time on his own he could hardly contain his excitement or his nervousness, almost forgot everything he had learned. And he only went down the road to the grocery store. But everybody was impressed, Mama, Etta, even Rebecca, although she didn't want to admit it. Charleston could drive. Now they wouldn't have to depend entirely on Papa.

ETTA

10

It was storming, the rain blowing sideways in sheets, the wind whipping the trees, bending their branches, stripping them of their leaves, the lightning flashing off and on like so many defective light bulbs, and the thunder clapping so loud it made your ears hurt. It had been threatening all morning, forcing the sun in and out of the darkening clouds and stirring up the light breeze. It was the kind of day that made me restless and on edge, unable to relax; the kind of day that terrified Becca - had her hiding in her bedroom closet, her hands over her ears. Only Mama was her usual calm self, working quietly at the dining table on a pattern, its papery pieces scattered over the shiny surface. If she was scared or worried about Papa and Charlie, who were on the road somewhere, she wasn't showing it, humming softly as she pinned and cut. I envied Mama.

During storms, I tried to distract myself, do something I dreaded, like straightening my closet or cleaning my drawers. I wandered to my bedroom, changed my mind, and tip toed into Mama and Papa's room. I turned on the radio, even though the house rule was when it was storming there was no telephone, no ironing, no cooking, and no radio. No nothing that might attract lightning's attention. I turned it down low, so low I could hardly hear. I pressed my ear against the speaker, holding my breath afraid the big scary t-word was going to be mentioned. When tornadoes were around, the day took on a certain kind of look, a different feel. The sky turned a weird greenish-tint and the air was still, so still, like it was holding its breath. At least it wasn't nighttime. It was worse then when the

43

electricity went out and the lightning lit up the rooms and thunder shattered the silence making sleep impossible.

"Turn off the radio, Etta," Mama shouted up the stairs.

The sound of her voice surprised me. I knew she couldn't hear it, but I should have known I couldn't fool her either. She knew me too well. I did as I was told and heard the back door slam, heard Papa and Charlie's voices, and felt safe. I always felt safe when Papa was home, like nothing bad could happen. I left their room and hurried down the hall past Becca's. Her door was ajar and the lights were on. I peeked inside. She was nowhere in sight. "Papa and Charlie are home," I yelled, assuming she was still shut up in the closet. There was no response. I pushed her door wide open just because and scrambled down the stairs to the kitchen.

"Thank God, you're home," Mama was saying, relief in her voice.

"We hadn't gotten on the road yet," Papa said, giving her a peck on the cheek, "the lights kept flickering in the office, so we decided to come home."

"Good, now I won't have to worry."

"I'm glad you're home, too, Papa," I said, giving him a hug.

"So am I, Etta, is your sister still hiding?"

I nodded.

"Poor Rebecca, I wish I could ease her fears."

"I think the closet does that. Where's Charlie?"

"Probably on the front porch where he shouldn't be," Mama said, handing Papa a steaming cup of black coffee. "He knows that's not safe, but he loves this kind of weather."

CHARLIE

11

    Charlie was on the porch sitting in the swing smoking, feeling the rain and wind on his face, listening to the loud claps of thunder and watching the squiggly fingers of lightning stretch across the dark sky, their manic flash brightening up its blackness. The rain was coming down in sheets; water was pooling in the grass and flooding the gutters. It was his kind of day. He loved storms. He could feel all that wild, raw energy surging through his body. Even as a little boy, when Mother Nature put on her show, he loved the lightning and thunder, the wind and the rain and wasn't frightened by any of it. He still wasn't.

    He heard the screen door squeak open and knew it was Etta. Mama was probably still in the kitchen with Papa, and Rebecca was probably still shut up in her closet. He remembered that from his growing up years. He never understood Rebecca's fear, couldn't relate to her being so frightened of storms.

    "Etta, come sit," he said patting the space beside him.

    "You shouldn't be out here, Charlie, it's not safe," she said, feeling the rain on her skin and the wind in her hair as she eased into the swing.

    He felt it sway and became aware of her scent.

    "It's just Mother Nature having her way again. It won't hurt you."

    "You could be struck by lightning."

    "Nonsense."

    "It's also a good way to catch cold,"

"Hardly, it's like being in a warm rain shower." He laughed and tossed his cigarette over the porch railing. "Rebecca's all closed up in her closet, right?"

"Everybody's not like you, Charlie."

"You are."

She shook her head.

"Admit it, Etta," he said, moving closer.

"Storms scare me," she said. "If you were honest, they probably scare you too."

"Not even a little bit."

"I don't believe you."

"Believe what you want." He laughed again started gently massaging her shoulder with his fingertips. Her skin felt smooth and moist and smelled of body lotion. He felt stirring in the pit of his stomach. He felt her body tense before pushing him away.

"You don't need to do that."

"Why are you afraid of my touch?"

"It feels weird."

"What do you mean, weird?"

"You're my brother," she said, wiping at her shoulder. "Or, maybe it's because you've been gone so long," she added, not wanting to hurt his feelings.

She looked at him. The rain was dotting his boy-man face with wetness and the wind was ruffling the collar of his shirt. He didn't say anything, just looked at her, but there was something in his look. Her stomach turned over. She needed to get away from his gaze.

He got up from the swing and walked to the railing, stared out at the rain. The wind seemed to be fading, the rain didn't seem as heavy and the lightning and thunder seemed to be moving away. He turned and looked at her again. She seemed so innocent, so full of possibilities. He watched her struggling out of the swing still wiping *away his touch.   Then she was gone, the screen door banging closed behind her.*

Had she seen the want in his eyes?   Was that why she left in such a hurry?   What was she thinking?   Would she mention it to Mama?   He sighed and sat back down on the swing.   What was there to mention?   He had only touched her shoulder.   He had to cool it, get his thoughts and feelings under control.   After all, she was still his sister whether she seemed like it or not.

ETTA

12

I couldn't get Charlie's look out of my head. It kept popping in and out of my mind. When I practiced the piano, his gaze would appear in the spaces between the notes on the sheet music and I'd feel his fingers on my shoulder. When I read a book, it was there among the words staring out at me from the pages. Of course, his gaze invading my dreams was a given. I couldn't figure out why it kept haunting me. As kids, we were always laughing and joking and touching. Maybe that was it. We weren't really kids anymore. I wanted to avoid Charlie at least for a while until I got my thoughts straight. I couldn't of course. He was my brother. We lived in the same house, ate at the same table, and rode in the same car. We were always around each other. I wanted to mention it to Becca. She was my big sister, I should have been able to, but Becca and I were not close. She acted like we were enemies instead of sisters, usually treated me like I was just someone to be tolerated. I was slowly realizing Becca treated most people like that and she was always complaining about Charlie being snooty and arrogant. He was, but so was she. I wanted to mention that, too, but figured she already knew. I briefly thought about going to Mama. Mama was very clear about us coming to her for anything no matter how small or silly. What would I say? Charlie looked at me and massaged my shoulder? We're siblings, what was wrong with that? But this felt different I wanted to tell her. I didn't. I was almost fifteen, no longer a little kid. I didn't need Mama to remind me. And, of course, it never entered my mind to mention it to Papa.

CHARLIE

13

Charlie had proven to be a good driver so Papa let him use the car whenever he didn't need it. He was kind of hoping Papa would buy him one, not a Packard, just some little non-descript used car like a Ford, but Papa seemed quite willing to share. Of course he had strict rules, no going beyond the posted limits, no smoking in the car ever and definitely no drinking. Charlie didn't complain. He loved the freedom and the fact he was no longer stuck at home like a prisoner. And unlike the other stuff he had gotten away with, he knew Papa was serious. One slip-up and his privileges were over.

Saturday evenings he would often drive to the college not far from town to listen to the band that played in a popular little club on campus. He knew Rebecca and Etta thought it was probably more to meet girls, but it was the band. The members were all students majoring in music. They were good. He was impressed and excited and wanted to join them. He finally approached the leader, mentioned he played the trumpet wondered if he ever thought about adding another instrument. The guy acted like he wasn't interested but Charlie kept talking, like only Charlie could, and talked his way into an audition. "That's all it took," he bragged. He got the gig. He was delirious, anxious to prove to Papa there was a future in music even though Papa had doubts. He was convinced that wouldn't be too hard. He was still Papa's favorite.

Papa and Mama reluctantly went to hear him play and had to admit he was good. They were proud of him. And he was so proud ofhimself he took Rebecca which surprised her and Etta. Rebecca actually had fun, which surprised Etta even more.

It only happened once, though. Charlie claimed having Rebecca along was a drag. The few colored girls on campus thought she was his date. Etta found that hard to believe since Charlie and Becca looked so much alike.

After he joined the band, he practiced all the time, keeping the house filled with mellow sounds. He still went to work with Papa everyday even though he had gotten what he wanted. The insurance business fascinated him. Like Papa, he was comfortable with people, charming, liked to talk, and had a good head for figures.

Papa was pleased and proud and bragged about Charleston following in his footsteps. Charlie never encouraged him, never made him think that might be a possibility.

"Remember, I'm only doing this for the summer, Papa. I'll be going back to college in the fall. I want to be a musician."

"I know, son, I know," Papa said, "but there's nothing wrong with having a little something extra in these hard times."

Mama just shook her head. "Jonas, let the boy be." She seemed to be resigned to the truth that music really was his life.

"I'm just saying, Anna, he might want to keep it as an option."

He was in the city with Papa at one of Papa's regional meetings. It met once a year usually in summer and was always held in the capital. The morning sessions were open to the public. The afternoon ones were private. Papa thought it would be a good learning experience and he would find it interesting. Charlie also suspected Papa just wanted to show off his son. The meeting was held in one of the large fancy hotels in the heart of downtown. The room was spacious and elegant and everyone was dressed in his Sunday best. There were no women and Papa was the only Colored man. The staff was professional and polite, but he wondered if he and Papa decided to spend the night if *they could get a room.*

Papa was right; the sessions were informative and interesting. Charlie left after lunch.

He was meandering around downtown passing time thinking of what to get Etta for her birthday. He was actually looking forward to her birthday. He remembered well how Mama always made birthdays a private celebration with special meals and spectacular cakes. He was still trying to decide what to get her. It had been easy when she was an awkward kid into books and writing pads and sheet music. She still was into books and writing and music, but they no longer seemed appropriate. She didn't seem like such a kid anymore as she moved through the transitional stage from adolescence into womanhood that he was finding so fascinating. He wanted his gift to reflect that.

Maybe he would ask Rebecca. He laughed out loud for even considering the idea. Rebecca and Etta seemed so out of sync that she probably wouldn't have a clue. Had they always been and he hadn't been interested enough to notice, or was this something new?

His memories of Rebecca were kind of vague. Nothing really special popped into his thoughts. She had always been smart and pretty and wrapped up in herself, but he didn't remember her being moody and sarcastic, almost obnoxious, like she seemed now. He wasn't too surprised though. The potential had been there and two years had changed all of them.

Or maybe he'd ask Mama. No, Mama would probably come up with something practical, something he was pretty sure would not be what he had in mind. He finally decided he would come up with something on his own.

As he stood looking at the displays in the shop windows, an idea popped into his head. He could take Etta on a shopping spree to the city, just the two of them. They could browse through all the big *stores and she could pick out something she really liked. They could have lunch at some fancy restaurant and spend the rest of the day exploring the city. They could go on a Saturday when Papa was off. He knew Papa would let him have the car. The more he thought about it, the more he liked the idea. It would be fun and exciting and Etta would love it. It would be the perfect gift.*

ETTA

14

The day of my fifteenth birthday I woke up early like my body knew it was my special day and wanted to get on with it. I lay still listening. The house was quiet. I slipped out of bed, walked to the window and peeked behind the shade. The pale half- moon was abandoning the clear sky. The branches on the big shade tree close to my window were swaying gently, their leaves flapping as if in some private celebration.

Fifteen! Suddenly fourteen seemed childish and immature. Why hadn't I noticed that before? Fifteen. Wow! I'd be in tenth grade when school started. I could start planning for college, maybe even learn how to drive.

I got back in bed but couldn't sleep. My mind was running amuck. Gifts dominated my thoughts. What would Mama and Papa give me? Along with a delicious meal of my choosing and a big fancy cake, there was always a gift, something smart and creative and personal. I could usually figure it out because I talked about it all year, especially the closer it got to my day. I always acted surprised even though I suspected Mama and Papa knew it was just an act. This year I wouldn't have to pretend. There wasn't anything I particularly wanted. What I did know was my usual smothered pork chops with mashed potatoes and gravy had beaten out Mama's fried chicken.

And what about Becca? I never knew about Becca. It depended on her mood. If she were in her egotistical selfish one, it wouldn't be anything at all. Charlie was another story. He usually went over board. He loved topping everyone else. I was curious what he would get me this year especially since he had been gone and seemed different. I had no clue. Charlie. I was relieved he was finally slipping back into his proper place as my older brother.

I dosed off. When I woke again, the sun was filling the window shade with brightness and the house had taken on its usual rhythms. I stretched and pulled the sheet over my head not yet ready to get up. I wanted to savor my birthday and make it last as long as possible. I heard a soft knock.

"Etta."

"I'm awake, Mama," I said, hopping out of bed and opening the door.

She was holding a tray loaded with food, a big smile on her face. "Happy Birthday."

I had forgotten that breakfast in bed and no chores were the other birthday perks. I scooted back under the sheet, smoothed the thin cotton material across my lap and shoved the pillows behind my back. Mama put the tray in front of me. All my favorites were there: buttery flaky pancakes, scrambled eggs and bacon, apple juice and hot cocoa. She gave me a kiss on the forehead and sat on the edge of the bed.

"How does it feel to be one year older?"

I sipped at the chocolate and grinned. "It really feels like I'm fifteen."

She laughed. "That's because you are."

"I mean it doesn't feel like yesterday I was fourteen. Well, I was but," I sighed. "I don't know how to explain it."

"You don't have to, sweetie. I think I understand. At your age, turning a year older is exciting. You're getting to the edge of adolescence, leaving it behind, becoming a young lady. I remember Rebecca couldn't wait, but you seemed in no hurry."

"I like being a kid. Becca's anxious to grow up."

"She's almost there and Charleston already has." There was a hint of sadness in Mama's voice. "You're all growing up so quickly, so, so fast." She smiled, gave me another kiss and got up from the bed. "You're only allowed to be a kid once, Etta, enjoy it." She tiptoed to the door and closed it behind her.

I really wasn't hungry but I ate the food anyhow, all of it. I didn't want to hurt Mama's feelings. I put the tray aside and hopped out of bed caught my reflection in the long mirror next to it. I looked at my self, twisting and turning trying to see what Charlie saw when he looked at me. Slowly I slipped out of my pajamas and stared at my naked body. My body had changed. There was fine kinky hair under my arms and sprouting between my legs and my breasts were no longer plastered against my chest. Hesitantly, I ran my hands over them lingering at the nipples and felt them harden; felt a funny tingling in my stomach. I moved my hands slowly past my belly button, picked at the hairs covering my private place, rubbed my hand over it softly, back and forth, back and forth. I closed my eyes and felt my breathing speed up. I stopped, afraid and ashamed like someone was watching. I put my pajamas back on quickly feeling guilty and a little dirty.

I was glad the kitchen was empty. Even after my bath, I was still feeling guilty and dirty and it probably showed on my face. I emptied the tray of the dishes, putting them in the sink, folded it up and stored it in its proper place. Through the wide glass windows, I saw Mama and Becca in the garden picking tomatoes and onions and carrots. I watched them for a while. Mama was talking and I could tell Becca was only half listening. There goes my present. I turned away. I hoped Papa and Charlie would be home early. Papa always tried to be home for birthday dinners. I was still curious about Charlie's gift. I felt it was going to be something different. No books or records or writing materials. This year I felt it was going to be something more personal.

"Happy Birthday to you, happy birthday to you," Becca was singing coming through the back door carrying a basket loaded with vegetables.

I laughed. It sounded like she meant it. She sat the basket on the counter and gave me a genuine smile. She didn't seem in a mood. It was just me.

"Thanks, Becca." I tried to give her a hug but she moved away to the sink and turned on the tap.

"Do you want your present now?" She was washing her hands not looking at me.

She had gotten me something. "I do but I can wait." It was usually our tradition we opened our gifts at dinner. Mama wasn't strict about it, though, kind of left it up to us. I remembered when Becca turned seventeen she had been so excited she had opened hers early. I was anxious, too, but liked the suspense of waiting, trying to guess what I had got.

"Suit yourself,' she said, drying her hands. "You haven't peeked at your cake have you?"

"Becca, I know that's a no-no." That was the other tradition. You didn't see your cake until dinner. I don't know why Mama had made up that rule.

"So what are you doing today?"

"I'm going to see Snow White and the Seven Dwarfs with Mavis and Angela. They're paying. You want to come?"

She shook her head. "That's for kids. Besides, I have to help Mama. Aren't you even a little curious about what I got you?"

"Do you want me to open it?"

"Why do you want to wait until dinner?"

"I like the suspense of not knowing."

"How ridiculous."

I shrugged. "Do you know what Charlie got me?"

"Why do you want to know about his gift and not mine?"

"You know Charlie. He always tries to outdo everybody."

"Well, I have no idea. Charleston doesn't seem to quite be himself lately."

"What do you mean?"

"Haven't you noticed he's . . . different."

Of course I'd noticed but I wanted to hear what she had to say. "Different how?"

"I don't know exactly. He's moody and antsy doesn't run his mouth so much. That's certainly not like Charleston."

She had described him perfectly. It wasn't just me. Charlie had changed. I wanted to tell Becca about the touching. She had admitted he was different. And I remembered the annoyance in her voice when he was staring at me.

"Oh well, he's becoming a man," she said flippantly, "that's probably what it is. He's out growing us."

I changed my mind.

Becca was right, it was a kid movie, but it was cute and fun and made me feel all happy inside.

"I loved the music," Angela said as we sauntered out of the theater.

"Me too." Mavis was taking off her glasses and fiddling with her hair. "We picked you a good birthday present, Etta."

"It was my choice, remember."

"At least we paid for it," Angela said.

"What are we going to do now?" Mavis asked still playing with her hair.

"Let's go for ice cream," Angela suggested.

I shook my head. "I can't."

"Mavis, did you hear that? Etta Netter doesn't want ice cream. She must be sick." She touched my forehead, "no fever."

"Funny." I pushed her hand away. "I don't want to spoil my dinner. Mama and Becca have been cooking all day and I'm sure Mama will have ice cream."

"Oops, I forgot, but it's kind of early to go home. It's your birthday. We should do . . . something."

"I know," Mavis said, finally freeing her hair, "let's go to the park."

"The park," Angela and I echoed.

"Yeah, we can go swimming. They rent bathing suits."

We stared at her.

"Have you forgotten coloreds can't swim in the pool?" Angela said.

"Sorry." Mavis's whole face was turning red and she was close to tears.

I felt bad for her but also a little mad. It must be nice to take things for granted.

"Besides, I can't swim," Angela added, grinning, trying to ease her embarrassment I guess. "Come up with something else."

"How about the library?" Mavis said, grinning too, but her face was still red.

We ended up at Angela's house talking, laughing and watching her younger brother Robert and two of his friends horsing around on their unicycles. Robert was cute and almost as shy as his sister. His friends were far from it. They put on quite a show. It was fun. Mavis and I talked and laughed about them most of the way home until she started apologizing for the swimming nonsense.

"It not your fault," I told her. "You didn't make up the stupid rule."

She smiled and gave me a big hug. "Happy Birthday, Etta."

My birthday dinner was perfect. Mama had made a centerpiece out of the huge bunch of colorful flowers Mavis's mother had bought over from her flower gardens. The pork chops smothered in gravy were delicious and the cake was fancy. Mama and Papa gave me a small solid gold heart dangling from a delicate gold chain with my initials engraved on the back.

"I hope you like it, Etta."

"I love it," I whispered, as Mama hooked it around my neck. "Thank you Mama. Thank you Papa."

"Open mine next," Becca ordered.

I picked up the big square box wondering what in the world it could be. I gave it a shake and heard a dull thud.

"Just open it."

I started peeling off the pretty wrapping grinning at her. It was a shoebox. Inside was a pair of beautiful black patent leather shoes with rounded toes and small heels and two pairs of silk stockings. I couldn't keep the surprise off my face. It was so unlike her. "They're beautiful," I said rubbing their shiny smooth surface softly with my fingertips.

"Mama and I agreed you're old enough to start wearing dress up shoes and hose," she said, pleased with herself.

"Thank you, Becca. Now, Mama will have to make me a pretty dress to wear with them."

"That's going to be my gift," Charlie said, "but I wanted you to pick it out. Something you like, something nice and pretty. We'll go shopping, just you and me, in the city."

"Wow, really Charlie?"

"I already have Papa's permission, right Papa?"

Papa nodded.

"Can't Becca go?"

I couldn't read the look that fleetingly crossed Charlie's face. "Sure, if she wants."

"You'll go won't you, Becca?"

She shrugged. "Depends on when you're going, Charleston?"

"On a Saturday when Papa takes a day off."

"Please go, Becca. It'll be fun."

"Okay, okay."

I glanced at Mama. There was a smile on her face and tears in her eyes. Her words about us growing up popped into my head. You're right Mama. I gave her a big open smile.

I tossed and turned, and couldn't sleep. I opened the window then closed it. I tried to read but couldn't concentrate. I turned on the light, turned it off. My birthday had been even more perfect than I expected and it wasn't over yet. I was going to the city with Becca and Charlie. How exciting would that be?

I couldn't wait. Every time I thought about it goose bumps popped out on my skin and I got excited all over again. But nothing was happening. I wanted to hound Charlie but didn't want to hurt his feelings. He had given me this absolutely perfect gift and I didn't believe him? How tacky and ungrateful would that be? So, I hounded Becca.

"I'm not Charleston," she said.

"I know, Becca, but I don't want to nag Charlie."

"Don't be silly, Etta, he's the one taking us."

But I was serious. I didn't want to nag Charlie. Instead, I nagged Mama.

"Etta, he said he was taking you, he will. You know your father and Charleston have been busy lately, be patient."

Mama didn't realize she was asking me to do the impossible. Patience was something I didn't have. Somebody, probably Becca, tipped Charlie off 'cause one day there was a note taped to my bedroom door in big bold letters, **I Haven't Forgotten.**

I chuckle. Patience. I still don't have any. It was something I never learned. Guess it's not in my nature. I finger the tiny gold heart dangling from the chain hanging around my neck. I've never taken it off not for seventy-one long years. It was so special, made me feel childish and sophisticated. Maybe that's how Mama saw me, a kid becoming a young lady. It's a constant reminder of Mama and Papa and my fifteenth birthday. I turn the little heart over and stare at my initials, rub them with my fingertips. They are smooth and worn and still define me. EMN, Etta Mae Netter. I will pass it to Francesca, the daughter who is not my daughter. I hope she will cherish it too. Maybe she'll even pass it to her daughter if she's blessed enough to have one.

CHARLIE

15

Charlie knew Etta was getting impatient. Rebecca had made that very clear. Even Mama had thrown out little hints, but there was nothing he could do. He and Papa were busy. The depression was finally easing. People were getting jobs back, getting paychecks and were eager to catch up. Papa's clientele was increasing. He started letting Charlie sell policies all on his own. He insisted on Charlie being honest and respectful, and he paid him ten percent for each one he sold. It helped but would have helped more if Charlie had his own car. Papa resisted the urge. Charlie liked selling. He also liked the fact he would have more money to spend when he did take Etta to the city. But they were busy and needed the car. It wasn't his fault. Etta would have to wait. To be honest, he was ticked at Etta. She really screwed up by asking Rebecca to go. The minute he heard her words he wanted to change his mind, take it back, just give her money to spend at J.C. Penny's or Sears or buy material for Mama to make her a new outfit. Rebecca wasn't in his plan. His plan was he and Etta alone together all day.

That she would even ask Rebecca never entered his mind. They really seemed to despise each other. He didn't think she would want to be stuck with her for a whole day. He kind of wondered if she asked because she didn't want to be alone with him or if she really wanted her to go? The more he thought about it, he had to admit it was understandable. Rebecca was her older sister. It was only natural she'd want to spend a day shopping with her, getting her opinion and sharing the fun. Besides, he hadn't given her any reason to be scared of being alone with him. It didn't matter. Rebecca was now part of the plan.

They finally went several weeks later, on a Saturday, of course. The day was clear and sunny but not hot. Charlie was relieved it wasn't raining. As much as he liked rain, he didn't like driving in it. It made the roads slippery, making him feel out of control. He left early. He wasn't sure about the traffic, wanted to spend as much of the day as possible shopping and exploring, and Papa insisted he be back before dark. So, he left just after sunrise before breakfast.

He liked the drive to the city. The road was flat and straight, fairly wide and in good condition. He liked driving through the middle of the small towns where he practically had to slow to a crawl, where the gas was cheaper and the tiny roadside stands were loaded with fresh fruits and vegetables and ice cold pop. He and Papa had been to the city so often he had gotten to know the route and the city well.

Etta sat up front in the passenger seat. Becca sat in the back behind Charlie. Etta had to admit she was impressed with Charlie's driving. He was attentive, kept his speed within the limits, and his eyes on the road. To be honest, at first she was a little scared, antsy about his driving skills, Becca probably was too, but he was a good driver, better than Papa, and there weren't that many cars on the road. There wasn't much to look at either, just occasional farmhouses, and fields and fields of corn. Becca kept up a steady stream of nonsense still mad at Papa.

"I don't know why Papa couldn't teach me too," she fussed.

"Let it go, Rebecca," Charlie said, "I'll teach you, okay."

"Ha, like Papa would let you."

"Do you want to learn or not?"

Rebecca didn't respond.

Charlie laughed. "I think you're scared," he said, glancing at her through the rearview mirror.

"You're not scared are you Becca?" Etta asked, twisting around in her seat to look at her.

63

"Of course not, I'd rather have Papa teach me that's all. He's been driving much longer than Charleston."

They couldn't argue with that.

Charlie concentrated on driving, half listening to Etta and Rebecca's chitchat. He wished Rebecca would shut-up about Papa and driving, but knew she was probably right; Papa wouldn't go along with his suggestion.

Every so often, he glanced at Etta, fought the urge to reach out and squeeze her hand. He was surprised she was so quiet. He figured she'd practically be jumping with excitement, but she seemed bored, staring out her window or turning in her seat to talk with Rebecca. She looked pretty in her black and white stripped sundress with the big black buttons down the front, skinny red belt and flat red sandals. Rebecca looked pretty too, in pink and white. He marveled at the contrast between them, Etta with her coco-brown skin looking like Mama and light-skinned Rebecca looking like him and Papa. He continued to look at Etta and got ticked all over again. It should have been just him and her. He sighed and shifted his attention back to the road.

Etta was bored, tired of sitting, and anxious to get there. The ride seemed longer than she remembered. When she started seeing more cars, she knew they were almost there and couldn't hide her excitement. Every time she came to the city it was like seeing it for the first time. The tall majestic insurance building, the gorgeous gold leafed dome of the old capitol, the noises, the cars, the street cars, even the people always caught her by surprise, practically taking her breath away. It was so different from their little town.

Charlie noticed Etta perked up, started fidgeting in her seat, and seemed to be on pins and needles the closer they got to the city. Rebecca seemed more alert too.

"I wondered when you were going to get excited."

"The first sight of the city always excites me," Etta said, glancing at her watch. "What are we going to do now, Charlie? It's too early for the stores to be open."

"I'm taking you to breakfast," he said, concentrating on the cars and the people crossing the street. Several of Papa's clients had gone on and on about a little hole in the wall restaurant in the Colored section they claimed served the best breakfast in town. He thought it would be fun to check it out, linger over good food laughing and talking and mapping out their day.

"Are you hungry?"

"How'd you guess? Are you hungry, Becca?"

"No."

"You can have something to drink, juice or tea or hot chocolate. You like hot chocolate," Etta said, twisting in her seat, again, to look at her.

"Or watch us eat," Charlie said, annoyed. Rebecca was already getting on his nerves.

"Not funny, Charleston, I should have stayed home."

I wished you had almost slipped out of his mouth.

"Oh come on, Becca," Etta said, wishing the same thing. "Think how much fun we're going to have shopping and looking around the city. You'll be glad you came." She refused to let Becca ruin her day. Why in the world had she begged her to come in the first place?

The restaurant was a little hole in the wall and they weren't sure they wanted to go in, but Charlie shrugged off Etta and Rebecca's doubts and sauntered through the screened door. It was small and crowded and noisy, but the smells made their mouths water and it was clean, charming in fact. The two long tables that ran down the middle of the room were covered with crisp red and white checked cloths that hung to the floor. Skinny high-backed caned chairs with white padded bottoms were pushed up under the tables. Breakfast was fantastic, light fluffy scrambled eggs and thick-sliced ham and crisp fried potatoes, biscuits and gravy and coffee like Charlie was used to in the South. The whole place reminded him of the South. All it lacked was the music. He loved it, enjoyed laughing and chatting with the folks around them. So did Etta. Even Rebecca couldn't resist. They stayed longer than they intended. And Papa's car was a big attraction. He loved that too, pretended it was his. For all they knew it was.

Their first stop was at The Grand Department Store downtown on Seventh and Walnut. It was new and huge, seven stories tall, and elegant. He thought Etta and Rebecca would get a kick out of it, have something to brag about to their friends and Etta should have little trouble finding a dress. He was glad he had extra money.

The store was intimidating. Etta and Rebecca stood staring, overwhelmed by its size. He followed them through the revolving glass doors and couldn't quite hide his amazement either, but tried hard. The store was big and fancy, and chaotic. Organized merchandise was all over everywhere,

"So, what do you think?" he asked, grinning.

"Wow, Charlie!" Etta said, looking around, wondering where the Coloreds were, wondering if they were even allowed. "Are you sure they let Coloreds shop here?"

"Don't be ridiculous," he said, "it's not the South."

They took the elevator to the girl's/women's department on the fourth floor. The sales people seemed to be mostly women, all white, of course. Some seemed fairly friendly or tried to be, others, seemed rude.

"Ignore them," Charlie said.

There were racks and racks of dresses in all colors, fabrics and patterns from cotton to crepe to gabardine, to plaid, striped, checkered, plain. From slim to full to straight, in all price ranges.

66

Charlie looked at Etta. She didn't seem that enthused anymore, which surprised him. She had been so looking forward to this shopping spree, but Rebecca was showing more excitement, going through the racks, commenting on what she liked and didn't like. Maybe it was just too much for Etta.

"What are you thinking?" he asked.

"How I'm going to pick just one."

Charlie laughed and started looking through the racks, pushing the dresses back and forth, pulling out the ones he thought she'd like. He was aware of the sales woman staring at them from across the room, offering no help. Stupid bitch.

"How do you like this one?" he asked, twirling it on its hanger in front of her.

The dress was pretty and her favorite color and would go good with the shoes Becca had gotten, but she didn't want it. She had lost her excitement about shopping.

"It's nice. What do you think, Becca?"

"I like it."

But she wanted to try it on see if it fit, how it felt, how it really looked against her skin. She couldn't. Coloreds weren't allowed.

Charlie glanced at the price tag dangling from the collar. The price was right. "Etta?"

"I wish I could try it on," she mumbled.

"Do you like it?" he repeated.

She looked at Charlie, looked at the silly white woman across the room and wanted to say no, keep the stupid dress she didn't want it. She didn't want any of them. She fought back her words. "Yes," she mumbled.

"We'll take it," Charlie said, walking toward the sales clerk. At first, she acted like she hadn't heard, then slowly started in their direction.

Etta watched the surprised haughty look forming on her face and changed her mind.

"On second thought, the color really doesn't do much for me, Charlie. What do you think, Becca?"

"Get it," Rebecca said, impatiently, looking at Charlie and rolling her eyes.

Etta could tell Charlie was upset but he put the dress back on the rack. She was suddenly mad at Charlie, Becca too.

"Let's try another store."

"Why didn't you let me buy it?" Charlie asked as they walked back to the car.

"I liked it a lot, Charlie, thanks, but it was the snooty clerk, even the store."

"You knew you couldn't try it on," Rebecca said, fussing and fuming all the way.

"I know, Becca, but she didn't have to treat us like dirt, act like we weren't even there. I changed my mind because I didn't want Charlie to give them his hard earned money."

"That's the way it is, Etta," Rebecca said. "It's going to be the same at the next store."

"Not if we go back to the Colored section."

Charlie had to give it to Etta. She held her ground with Rebecca, refused to be intimidated, and he liked her suggestion.

They went back and found all kinds of dress shops not quite as big or elegant but the clerks were nice and pleasant and helpful and looked like them. Etta tried on dress after dress, twisting and turning in front of long mirrors feeling the soft fabrics against her skin, watching them swirl around her legs putting on a show for Becca and Charlie. Charlie was engrossed, couldn't believe she was his baby sister. She finally picked one almost as pretty as the one at the white store and it cost less, so Charlie even brought Rebecca something.

They stayed in that part of the city surprised by all the things there were to see and do. It was fun and different and exciting. They walked around the beautiful private white university Papa said they'd built in the Colored section because the land was cheaper. They ate a fancy lunch at the colored Eagleton Hotel and had trouble dragging Charlie away from music stores. They lingered in small shops that sold jewelry and fabrics that didn't look like anything they had seen before, strange smelling fragrances, dressy hats and shoes. Charlie drove through neighborhoods where the colored people with money lived, laughed at Etta's and Rebecca's reactions to the elegant big houses and wondered, too, why Papa had never showed them that part of the city.

On the way home, Charlie stopped at a little roadside shack that had the best fried chicken they had ever tasted better even than Mama's. They bought some to take with them to see what Mama thought. It ended up being fun after all and having Rebecca along hadn't been as much of a drag as he'd thought. They barely managed to get home before dark.

But, next time, Charlie thought, it would be just him and Etta. He'd make sure of that.

ETTA

16

It was one of those hot lazy days of summer. The house was quiet. Mama and Papa and Becca were out buying all the stuff that didn't grow in the garden like meat and eggs and butter and bread and spices. I was surprised Becca went, but she was whining about being bored so Mama suggested she go along. I was bored, too, but didn't have the patience or desire for grocery shopping. Charlie was probably also bored. It was that kind of day, but he was in his room practicing his trumpet, the sound of 'My Funny Valentine' filtering softly through the open windows and doors. I was lying in the swing on the front porch, mouthing the words and day dreaming about our trip to the city. I couldn't get over how fun and exciting it had been even with Becca along. Becca had grudgingly admitted she had fun too. We still laughed over the tacky little restaurant with the delicious food and Charlie trying to impress people with Papa's car and Mama's disagreement about the chicken. No way was it better than hers. And I still loved the dress Charlie bought me. I had worn it several times and got lots of compliments. Each time I put it on; I fell in love with it all over again. It was pretty and sophisticated and made me feel grown-up. I was afraid Mama wouldn't like it, but she did.

I shoved all those thoughts to the back of my mind and tried to concentrate on a poem that was stuck in my head, refusing to come together. The day was hot and humid and sticky. There was no breeze. Every now and then, I gave the swing a push with my bare foot making it sway. Slowly, it came to a stop forcing me to give it another. I had on shorts Mama had made from some baggy old pants and a sleeveless frilly white blouse that used to have long full sleeves with cuffs until I snagged one. Mama insisted it was still wearable and the fabric was too good to throw away. She cut off the sleeves. I kept tugging at it and my shorts, twisting and turning, changing positions, trying to stay cool. I was also gulping Mama's delicious lemonade hoping to satisfy my thirst. That wasn't working either. I had already emptied one tall full glass and still wanted more. I leaned out of the swing, took a jagged piece of ice from the empty glass sitting on the worn wooden floor and started rubbing it over my bare arms and legs ignoring its drippy messiness. The cold felt good against my hot skin but the ice melted quickly making it useless. I sat up, wiped my hands on my shorts and started fanning myself with my thick writing pad.

CHARLIE
17

Charlie was bored. He was missing the south with its slow lazy rhythm, his classmates, the girls and the music. His summer was turning out to be as dull and unexciting as he knew it would be. Even though he and Papa were busy selling insurance, boredom had become an ongoing part of his days, especially on weekends when Papa was busy chauffeuring Mama around, making the car unavailable. He had to admit though, Papa was generous with his car, but Charlie still wished he had his own and the thought of buying one popped into his head off and on, especially now that he was getting paid. He could probably get a used one, cheap. Then, he wouldn't have to depend on Papa's. He could even save Papa some money and drive back to college. It would be neat to have a car on campus. The more he thought about it the more he liked the idea. Yeah, he would have to work on it . . . and Papa.

He was hot, too, and miserable. He had forgotten how much like the South a Midwest summer could be with its heat and humidity. It made him sluggish and lazy and cut down on his running. He hadn't run since high school, but had started again on weekends, afraid of gaining weight from all Mama's good cooking. On hot humid days, though, he stuck to less strenuous activities like playing his trumpet.

He wiped the sweat off his lips and placed the trumpet back in its case. He wished he were a reader like Etta, but storybooks didn't hold his attention. He wandered downstairs to the kitchen, stood staring in the icebox looking for something to drink. He couldn't believe he and Etta were home alone. Rebecca was usually hanging around somewhere, but she had actually gone to the store with Papa and Mama, leaving him practicing his music and Etta writing on the porch. He wondered what he had done to deserve such good luck. He took out the lemonade, figuring Etta was probably as hot and miserable as him, chipped off some ice and put it in the bottom of one of Mama's fancy pitchers. He filled it up with the pale liquid, floated thin lemon slices on top, put the pitcher and a glass on a tray and headed for the porch.

"God, you look hot," he said. Her skin was shiny with sweat and the edges of her kinky hair were curled against her head. He sat the tray on a table and refilled her glass.

"That's because I am," she said. Why hadn't she thought of that? And how did Charlie manage to look so cool and crisp in his full cotton pants rolled up past his ankles, sleeveless undershirt and bare feet?

"I figured you were running on empty."

"Thanks, Charlie, you're a lifesaver." She took a swallow and tried not to gulp it, making him laugh.

He hadn't seen much of Etta since they got back from their trip, which seemed like a long time ago, but images of her twirling in front of the long mirrors, her girl-woman body looking so enticing in all the dresses she tried on, still popped into his head. He was pleased she had such good taste. He was already thinking about where they could go next, but he and Papa were still busy driving up and down the highway from dawn to dusk. By the time they got home, he was worn-out tired. He picked at Mama's dinners, took quick baths, sipped his nightly drinks with Papa and hit the sack. He didn't smoke a cigarette or think about his trumpet. He had even put playing in the band at the college temporarily on hold. He kept hoping their ceaseless travel would soon stop or at least slow down.

Not Papa. "When opportunity knocks, Son, you got to grab it," he insisted.

"I know Papa."

He poured lemonade into his glass and eased down beside her. "You're wet," he said, liking the feel of her moist skin.

"It's just ice, Charlie. I'm trying to keep cool."

"That doesn't work."

"It does for a little while."

"I know something that really works."

"Yeah, right." She saw that look in his eyes.

"I'm serious."

"How can you be so sure?"

"Do you know how hot it gets in Tennessee?"

"What's that got to do with anything?"

"Because it gets so hot your body can explode."

She laughed. "Quit lying."

"Well, maybe not that hot," he said, grinning, draining his glass and putting it on the floor.

She knew Charlie was lying but was curious and he knew it.

"How do you keep from exploding?" she asked, still laughing.

"It's called tactile stimulation."

"Wow, that sounds . . . scientific."

"Not really."

"What does it mean?"

"Touch."

"You can keep your body from getting too hot by just touching it?

He nodded. "Have you ever had a massage?"

"No, have you?"

"Yea, and the movement of hands over muscles relieves the stress and tiredness even the pain, totally relaxing the body. It's fantastic. Stimulating the skin with touch can have the same effect."

"I'm not sure I believe that."

"Give me your arm."

74

"Why?"

"Just give me your arm, Etta."

"Is this a trick?"

He shook his head.

She stretched out her arm. He took it, held it lightly, started moving his fingers softly, slowly, up and down, up and down.

"That tickles."

"Try to relax."

His fingers felt like tiny ants crawling all over her skin giving her goose bumps. She pushed them away.

"What's wrong?"

"It feels like bugs."

"You've got to relax, Etta," he said, rubbing her arm, again, this time with the flat of his palm barely touching creating the tiniest breeze between the gaps making her skin tingle. He slowly, so slowly, moved his touch up her arm to her shoulder, gave it a gentle squeeze, let his fingers play briefly around her neck before moving his hand back down her arm. "Feels good, right?"

She closed her eyes and sucked in her breath. It did feel good or maybe it was just in her head, but she didn't want him to know. She didn't respond.

"Told you," he said, reading her mind.

"I'm still hot."

"Give it time." He moved his body closer and saw Papa's car turning into the driveway. Damn.

"Why did you quit?" she asked, squinting at him.

"They're back. Papa will probably need help with the groceries."

"But, I'm still hot."

"I'll have to keep working on that," he said, suspecting she didn't really believe touching cooled the body.

ETTA

18

It stayed hot and sticky and unbearable with no breeze. At bedtime, I pushed my bedroom window up as high as it would go, hoping to catch any wisp of air that might blow through. Maybe the mosquitoes wouldn't realize it was open. I took a bath, rubbed Mama's smelling lotion over my arms and legs, put on clean pajamas. I fluffed up my pillows, plopped down on the cool sheets, closed my eyes and felt Charlie's soothing touch all over my hot body.

It was washday. Papa rolled the awkward Maytag wringer washing machine away from its allotted space against the wall on the back porch. He placed a sturdy wide wooden board behind it, put two large tin tubs side by side on top and filled them all up with water from the rubber hose attached to the tap of the kitchen sink, hot for the washer, cold for the rinse tubs. Later, Mama added Bluing. Mama swore by Bluing. She insisted it made the white clothes whiter and helped the coloreds keep their brightness. I hated washday, hated the washing, rinsing, hanging the clothes on the line, really hated putting them through the wringer. The wringer scared me. If the clothes got stuck between the rollers it made a loud whining noise wrapping them tighter and tighter and shaking like it was having a fit. Becca almost got the tips of her fingers caught between the rollers once, so now I was overly cautious putting the clothes in slowly, flat and even, and one piece at a time. The other thing I hated was emptying the water. The washer wasn't too bad. At least it had an attached hose. The tubs didn't. The water had to be dipped out into a bucket and carried to the bathroom. I couldn't wait until Mama got the new machine they kept bragging about on the radio, a Bendix Automatic they called it. There was even a picture in the newspaper. Mama talked about it all the time, put it at the top of the things she wanted most list and started taking in extra sewing.

"Imagine wash day made easier," she sighed.

That was way beyond my imagination. Until Mama actually got one, I continued to hate washday.

This washday was no different. Mama got up early, as usual, to get a head start and have breakfast with Papa. She always said having breakfast with Papa was the only good thing about washday and it was Friday, which meant changing the sheets and pillowcases and light blankets. Becca and I and Charlie stripped off our bedding and carried it down stairs to the porch where Mama washed in summers. During the winter, Papa dragged everything into the kitchen.

Becca was already grumbling even though Mama had let us sleep a little later. I didn't mind getting up early. Washing was a pain, but I liked getting up with the sun. It seemed to stretch out the day, and after we finished there was still time to read, or practice the piano, or work on a poem, or just do nothing, before we had to help with dinner.

The day was perfect, hot and breezy. The wind whipped the sheets free of wrinkles, drying them in no time. Becca could almost press them with her hands. She had taken the pillowcases off the line while they were still damp, rolled them in a thick towel and let them sit awhile. That eliminated sprinkling, she said, made the moistness more even, making them easier to iron. Although she fussed, Becca was a good ironer and the finished products looked like she enjoyed it. My chore was putting everything back. I loved it, loved flapping the fresh smooth sheets and thin blankets over the stripped beds tucking them tight underneath the thick mattresses, folding them neatly at the corners and slipping the goose down pillows into their crisp white cases. They smelled fresh and airy with a hint of bluing. I also polished the furniture, dusted the floors, and opened the windows. Becca couldn't understand why I did all that extra work as she called it. She couldn't believe I did it just because, but that was Becca. She loved being contrary.

I wondered how she was going to do at college, not in her studies, but in her acquaintances. She wasn't out going, didn't take easily to people. Making friends was hard work. I think Mama worried about that too.

Although Becca and I weren't the best of sisters, we were sisters, and every now and then she surprised me by being nice. Like once when I was sick she brought me hot tea, helped with my bath, changed my sheets and gave me back rubs, read to me for hours. I loved the closeness and wished she was always like that. When I got better and tried to thank her, she ignored me.

"Why can't you be nice all the time, Becca?"

"That would be boring," she said.

Even though I kept thinking I would be glad when she left, I was going to miss her.

And then there was Charlie. He was really into that tactile stimulation stuff. Every time we were alone, he was touching my arms, squeezing my shoulders, tickling my neck, even stroking my thigh. I had to admit; it wasn't cooling, just made goose bumps rise all over my skin.

Charlie.

My feelings for him were beginning to confuse me. He was my brother, but when we were alone, just the two of us, he didn't seem like it. He was so sophisticated smoking his cigarettes, drinking his liquor and blowing on his trumpet, he seemed more like some vaguely familiar person I was a little shy of but still curious about, curious enough to want to get to know better. And I'll admit I was beginning to like all his attention. I didn't have a boyfriend, but suspected this was the way one would make me feel, all excited and cute and grown-up-special. Funny, when we were around Papa, Mama, even Becca, I could hardly stand him, hated his staring or when he gave me that look. I didn't understand that either. Yeah, I was becoming totally confused about Charlie. One day I wanted to tell somebody. The next day I didn't. I kept wondering why me?

I finally got up the nerve to ask.

He didn't answer just stared at me.

"Why, Charlie?" I repeated.

"I told you," he said, "when I left, you were a kid, a skinny all arms and legs annoying kid. Now you're . . ."

"Still a kid."

"That's not what I see."

"I'm fifteen."

"But I look at you and see . . ."

"What? What do you see?"

"Etta, Etta, Etta, how can I explain? I see a very pretty girl at the beginning of womanhood, a girl not yet aware of her beauty or her sexuality, her effect on . . ."

"I'm your sister," I interrupted, needing to block out his words.

"That's just it, Etta, you don't seem like my sister. You're more like some stranger I want to get to know better."

He didn't need to say anymore. He had said exactly how I felt about him.

"I'm still your sister," I repeated.

Charlie was getting to be more than I could handle. I needed to tell someone, not Becca and certainly not Papa, Mama, maybe, or my best friend, Angela. I pushed the thought out of my mind. I really couldn't imagine telling any of them. Then, I remembered the pretty little pink satin diary with the tiny silver key Mama had given me for one of my birthdays. There was only one entry in the entire book, something I had written about a school trip, nothing special. I don't know why it was in there. I always thought diaries were for personal stuff, stuff you didn't want anybody else to know. I wondered at the time why Mama had given it to me. Now, I was glad. It was perfect for writing down my confused thoughts and feelings, even if I didn't have the words to describe them.

It became my secret. I started writing in it practically every day, usually in the swing on the porch when no one was around, or at night after my bath in my bedroom behind my closed door. It was about Charlie, of course - his looks, his touch, his words - words I sometimes didn't understand -, whispered in my ear.

It was about his first hesitant kiss, his lips, opened, the tip of his tongue teasing mine, tightly clamped and closed - taking me by surprise, making my head spin and my ears pound, his voice asking if I liked it. It was about me lowering my head refusing to look at him and him lifting my chin, pressing his lips against mine, again.

It was about his hands and fingers accidently or on purpose brushing against my breasts and nipples making them harden and tingle through the soft cotton fabric of my tops and starting that funny good feeling in my stomach. It was all about Charlie and me and innocence and curiosity and coming of age and sexual awakening.

I worried what Mama or Papa even Becca would do if they happened to get a hold of my secret writings. Would they think it was just make believe or would they think it was real, Charlie and me behaving like boyfriend and girlfriend? What would they do to me, to Charlie? I didn't want to find out so I always made double sure it was locked and the key was hidden.

CHARLIE

19

Charlie was glad Papa's business had slowed and they were back on their regular schedule. He went back to practicing his trumpet, started running again and playing in the band at the college. His cigarette consumption increased and he once again enjoyed his evening drink with Papa. And he concentrated on seducing Etta. He thought she seemed more comfortable, more relaxed, no longer moved away from his touch. He kept pushing his luck. When she was in the swing on the porch, he would ease down beside her and stroke her arms. When she practiced the piano, he'd sneak up behind her and massage her shoulders. When they were in the car, and Papa was driving, he'd managed to sit beside her instead of Rebecca, stretch his arm out against the back of the seat and tickle her neck with his fingers. Occasionally, he went with her to the library, bought her ice cream Sundays at Kresege's five and dime, laughed and chatted and teased her like they were courting.

He was becoming obsessed with Etta. She haunted his dreams and messed with his mind, distracting him. Papa was beginning to notice.

"Something bothering you, son?" he asked after Charlie made two wrong turns on the way to a client's house.

He shook his head. "Why are you asking?"

"Well, we've been to old Samuel's place before and this is the second time you've missed his turn off."

Charlie tried to laugh it off. "I'm tired that's all. It's been a long, hectic day."

"You're sure right about that."

"My concentration's a little bit off."

81

"I thought something might be troubling you."

"I'm fine, Papa."

"All right, then, but I'm just saying if you need to talk . . ."

"I'm fine," he repeated, "especially now that you've quit working me so hard."

Papa laughed.

Charlie wanted to kick himself. That's all he needed, Papa getting curious about his business, especially now when he was trying to get more involved with Etta. He started sitting next to her at the dinner table and went with her on walks around the neighborhood. He usually asked Rebecca to come along or Mama, even Papa. He didn't want it to seem obvious. He had never paid much attention to their neighborhood. He was pleasantly surprised at the pretty old houses with their manicured lawns, colorful flowers, numerous fruit trees and large vegetable gardens. Sometimes, Mama did go, stopping to chitchat with the neighbors, enjoying her self.

Afterward, he and Etta sat on the porch in the swing and he told her about the South.

"It's different from here, Etta."

"How different?"

"There are so many places colored people can't go like restaurants and stores and movie houses, which is ridiculous. On the positive side, they have their own neighborhoods, businesses, doctors, lawyers, schools and teachers. Do you know there are only a handful of white students and teachers at my college?"

"That is different. Do you like it?"

"Yeah, I do. It is different and it took me a while to adjust to some of it, but yeah, I like it."

"Think Becca would?"

Charlie laughed. "I can't even imagine Rebecca in the south. She'd be totally out of her element. She could never get used to southern ways."

"I'm not sure I could either."

"Yeah, you could. Like I said, it just takes some getting used to.

Etta sighed and gave the swing a push with her foot. "You'll be going back before long."

He didn't respond. The only sound was the loud rhythmic squeaking of the swing. "Are you going to miss me?" he asked, looking at her.

"Don't be silly, Charlie, of course I'll miss you, Becca too."

"What will you do here all by yourself?"

"I won't be by myself. There's Mama and Papa and my friends Angela and Mavis, and school will keep me plenty busy. And, hopefully, Papa will teach me how to drive."

"God, Rebecca will truly have a fit if you learn before her."

Etta laughed.

"Speaking of driving," he said, grinning, "I'm thinking of buying a car."

"Really?"

He nodded, still grinning. "I'm tired of having to depend on Papa's."

"You have that much money?"

"Enough to get a used one, I think."

"How neat. What does Papa say?"

"I haven't mentioned it to him yet."

"Good luck."

"If I had my own car, it would save him money and gas and I could drive it back to college saving him more money."

"Sounds great."

"I could, Etta, and it would be so cool to have a car on campus."

"Charlie, it's Papa you have to convince."

She gave the swing another push and felt a wave of sadness engulf her.

He wasn't having any luck convincing Papa about the car, which caught him off guard, again. He still wasn't used to Papa not giving in to his every whim. But as with the driving, Papa was sticking to his guns.

"It's not about buying a car, son. It's driving it South. You don't know the ways of the South," he argued. "You might think you do. But you don't."

"I've lived in the South for two years, remember? I know how ridiculous those people can be."

"Lived there, yes. You haven't driven there. Trust me. That's a whole other experience."

"How do you know, Papa?"

"I've done it, several times and it was hell every time. I don't want you to go through it. It's not safe, especially for a young colored boy driving by his self."

"I know about segregation."

"Knowing about, it and facing it head on, is two different things. Just imagine what you would do if you couldn't find a place to stay after driving all day or couldn't buy gas when your tank's hovering on empty, or get something to eat when your stomach's growling. That's what you can expect and worse driving through the South."

The more Papa talked, the more Charlie listened. He knew Papa was telling the truth. "I still think a car of my own is a good idea," he grumbled.

84

"I agree, Charleston. Maybe when you come home next summer, we'll look into it."

Next summer sounded like forever. All kinds of things could happen by then but Papa had a point. Besides, time had a way of flying like it seemed to be doing now. It hadn't been that long ago he was complaining about boredom and time dragging, practically standing still. No longer. Soon summer would be turning into fall and he would be heading back to college. He wasn't in a hurry to leave. He had gotten comfortable being home, again. He was going to miss driving up and down the highway with Papa, learning how to sell insurance, Mama's cooking, Rebecca's sarcasm and Etta's everything. He was actually going to miss being home.

ETTA

20

The days continued to be hot and humid, almost unbearable, cooled only by the rainstorms full of lightning and thunder that erratically passed through. Tornadoes were all over the state but luckily none hit our town. Some came close enough for their winds and rains to cause creeks and rivers to overflow, flooding low areas, like the park where our annual church picnic was held, causing it to be cancelled.

Summer was flying. It seemed only days since Charlie got home, and my birthday was now just a fun-filled memory except when I wore the dress or shoes Charlie and Becca had given me. We hadn't been back to the City. Mama and Papa went, but Charlie, Becca, and I chose to stay home. I think Charlie was hoping Becca would go, but she never did. She was spending more and more time getting ready for college, although she didn't seem in as big a hurry as she claimed. And whether she admitted it or not, she was going to miss us, at least Mama and Papa.

Charlie would be leaving, too, but he didn't act like it. He still went to work with Papa every day, still tried to talk Papa into buying a car, still played at the college on Saturday nights and when we were alone, still treated me like his girlfriend. I was getting used to Charlie and no longer felt guilty. So what if we were sister and brother? It wasn't as if we were doing anything. Sometimes he teased about putting his private part into my private part, but I didn't take him seriously. It was just a tease. It was mostly kissing, fondling, and every now and then him putting his fingers between my legs. Once, when Mama and Papa were in the city and Becca had taken the bus to Main Street, he slipped his fingers into my private part, stroking something that made my stomach cramp like just before my monthly bleeding started making me feel like I was going to throw up. Instead, my body began twisting and turning moving with his movements. My heart started racing and I could hardly breathe. I pushed his fingers away and felt wetness.

"Congratulations, Etta," he whispered, "You've just experienced an orgasm."

I heard his voice but couldn't understand what he was saying. My mind was too confused trying to figure out what had just happened, why my body felt so different, not like my body at all.

"Did you hear me, Etta?" He was still whispering, nibbling on my ear. "You've just had an orgasm."

I ignored his words. My body felt dirty and I wondered if it smelled. I needed to get away from him. I pushed him away, hurried to the bathroom and turned on the water in the tub. I started pulling at my blouse, shorts, brassier and underpants. My fingers didn't want to work, felt like all thumbs, like they were moving in slow motion. I managed to get them all off, but couldn't wait for the tub to fill. I put my foot in the too hot water, quickly turned the cold tap on full.

I soaked in the tub hoping the water would cleanse me. The orgasm word kept running thru my mind. Orgasm. What a funny sounding word, orgasm, sounded almost like organ. Did it have anything to do with music? It had certainly created a rhythm in my body making me dance to Charlie's movements. Orgasm, I had never heard the word before and didn't know what it meant, only how it had made me feel.

Who could I ask? Who would talk about orgasm? Not Becca. She had never even had a boyfriend, neither I suspected, had Angela or Mavis. What about Mama? Did Papa give her orgasm? If he did, why didn't she ever talk about it? It had to be a no-no. I heard the bathroom door squeak open. As always, I had forgotten to lock it. Charlie was peeking around its corner.

"Are you all right, Etta?"

"Leave me alone, Charlie."

He stared at me before closing the door.

I couldn't get the word out of my mind. I spent days at the library trying to find it in the dictionary but wasn't sure how to spell it and didn't want to ask. I stumbled across a book on the human body called Gray's Anatomy that had lots of information even ink pen drawings of body parts with their names printed neatly underneath. I was fascinated, greedily soaked up the words, and stared at the pictures. I wanted to check out the book but was afraid of what the librarian would think. I kept going back, getting the book off the shelf and engulfing myself in it. I didn't understand most of it. I kept reading and rereading trying to comprehend what it was saying, copied words, phrases, even sentences in my school notebook to struggle over later at home in my bedroom behind closed doors. And of course, I wrote about it in my diary.

I thought about telling Angela again, but I hadn't seen much of her lately. Her mother was working more days and longer hours and she was stuck at home babysitting. Every time I thought about telling her, I changed my mind. Angela was religious like her mama and papa and more sheltered than me, if that was possible. I couldn't imagine her knowing anything about orgasm. Besides, I was too ashamed to ask.

CHARLIE

21

Charlie hadn't planned it, was almost as surprised as she when it happened. It was one of those rare occasions when they had the house to themselves. He was working on some forms Papa was hounding him about finishing. Paper work was the one thing he hated about the insurance business. For every client he signed up, there were tons of forms to fill out and he always let them go until Papa got on his case. His focus was on getting them done to get Papa off his back. The house was quiet. He worked at the kitchen table enjoying the warmth of the sun on his skin through the wide windows. She wasn't even on his mind for a change. He knew she was upstairs in her bedroom cleaning out her desk drawers, at least that's what she had said, promising not to disturb him.

He finished the last of his paper work and glanced at his watch. It was close to noon. He was hungry, wondered if she was too, decided to fix sandwiches for lunch. He got out the thick sliced whole wheat bread, the cold left over roast beef and the coarse grain mustard. He spread mustard on two slices of bread, carved the meat thin, piled it high on top, and covered it with the rest of the bread slices. He placed them on paper plates with fat dill pickles, grabbed some paper napkins and went upstairs.

"Lunch is ready," he said, pushing her door wide open.

She was stretched out on the bed reading.

"Great," she said, sitting up, pushing the pillows against the headboard and easing against them. "I'm starving."

He grinned and handed her both plates.

"Hmm, they look delicious."

He plopped down beside her, took back one of the plates, put it on his outstretched legs and took a bite.

"Are you finished with your work?" she asked, taking a bite of hers too.

"All finished." He swallowed and took another bite. "Oops, I forgot to bring something to drink."

"You'd make a poor waiter," she said, grinning, "but the sandwich is delicious."

"Would you rather have a delicious gourmet sandwich or something to drink?"

"Both, but I'll take the sandwich."

"What are you reading?" he asked, peeking at her book.

"Little Women," she said, wiping her mouth with the napkin, putting it and the empty plate on the floor.

"That hasn't changed."

"What?"

"Keeping your head in a book."

She laughed. "I love books."

"What else do you love?" he asked, putting his used napkin and empty plate on the floor too.

"Hearing you play your trumpet."

"I love playing it." He scooted closer.

She eased off the pillows and rested her head on his shoulder. "I know."

"How do you know?" he asked, rubbing her bare leg.

"You can hear it in your music."

"Really?" He moved his hand farther up her thigh, slipped it under the wide leg of her shorts and turned on his side toward her.

"Really." She closed her eyes; aware of his hand and felt goose bumps popping up all over her skin.

90

He worked his fingers under her panties; felt her baby soft skin, the short prickly hairs, slipped a finger into her opening and found the tiny nub, started moving his finger slowly back and forth and around. He felt it stiffen, felt him stiffen, heard her moan and felt her body shudder.

"You've just had an orgasm, Etta." He knew it had scared her. He wanted to relieve her fears, try to explain, but she was already out of the bed and running toward the door. He followed her to the bathroom, heard the water running, heard her sobs. He turned the doorknob; surprised it was unlocked, and peeked around its edges.

"Etta."

"Leave me alone, Charlie."

He stared at her. God, he wanted her. It was that simple. But, he was scared, wasn't sure he wanted to take such a bold step. He wasn't even sure how far he could go before she rebelled. It would just be his luck to get caught or she would finally tell. He gave her one last look and closed the door.

ETTA

22

Charlie and I were spinning out of control. The touching was getting more forward and starting to develop into something else. It wasn't just arms and legs anymore. It was more frequent kisses, his hands slipping inside my blouse fondling my breast and his fingers circling my nipples. His finger between my legs was becoming more insistent too. I tried to resist, keep it where it had been, but whenever he ventured into new territory, I shivered, my stomach flipped, and my body tingled with pleasure. Confusion and guilt were now my constant companions. I didn't know quite where it was headed, but suspected Charlie did.

Maybe it was me, but our household felt like it was spinning out of control, too. Becca had become obsessed with college, was practically in a panic running around like a chicken with her head cut off. She was separating her books, going through her closets trying to decide what clothes to take and which to leave behind, what needed cleaning, mending, what shoes needed soles or heels, or to be thrown away. Mama even got caught up in her obsession, frantically sewing new dresses, and skirts, and blouses, making me wish I was the one leaving.

Papa and Charlie were in their own frenzy, again, working all day Saturdays and often on Sundays, which made Mama mad. Sundays were her days; we often heard her yelling at Papa. Charlie wasn't happy either. It messed with his band playing, but Papa's clientele had increased. Colored folks had always bought life insurance, Papa said cause it was a cheap safe way to provide for their families after they were gone. And Papa was a professional, went out of his way for his clients. He kept reminding Mama extra money was always welcomed and teased her about getting her automatic washing machine quicker. Mama couldn't argue with that, but still she wasn't pleased.

Our whole household seemed to be running amok.

That Charlie wasn't around much or was tired when he and Papa finally got home was a big relief. So, he caught me completely off guard one night when he slipped into my bed waking me from a sound sleep. I have to admit, I was dreaming about him, his minty breath against my neck, the smell of his shaving cream drifting through my nostrils, the length of his warm hard body pressed flat and tight against my backside. I'm not sure when I realized it was no longer a dream. Confused and disoriented, I opened my eyes, recognized my window shade with its fancy fringe, the pale yellow wallpaper with the tiny blue flowers, my books scattered on the floor. It was my room. It had to be my bed. What was he doing in it?

"Charlie?"

CHARLIE

23

He knew he was taking a chance. Rebecca, Mama even Papa might see him sneaking into her room in his underwear, but he didn't care. Ever since the day of her orgasm he had decided he would have her, take his chances of getting caught or of her telling. His obsession with her was killing him. He was willing to take the risk.

He left his room as soon as the house was quiet, afraid of losing his nerve. He stopped in front of Rebecca's door. It was slightly ajar. He could hear her steady rhythmic breathing. He tiptoed down the hall to Mama and Papa's room and leaned his ear against their closed door, heard only the sound of Papa snoring. He tiptoed back to Etta's.

That she never locked her door amazed him. She might be coming into womanhood but she was still an innocent. That's what fascinated him. Ever so slowly he opened her door, relieved it didn't squeak, closed it quietly and stood still adjusting to the darkness. She was lying on her side facing away from him. The thin sheet was pushed down past her waist covering only her legs. She was breathing quietly, her chest moving in and out, slow and even. Her pajama top was hiked up exposing smooth brown skin.

He felt his fullness as he moved toward the bed, eased down and stretched out his body. He laid still, closed his eyes and breathed in her scent. He inched closer and closer, until their bodies met.

She stirred.

He stopped, waited, then put his hand under her top cupping one small breast running a finger across the nipple.

She stirred again, flinging her arm against his face, becoming aware of his presence. She turned toward him with a confused look in her eyes.

ETTA

24

"Charlie?"

I sat straight up pulling the covers tight around me. My heart started beating fast pounding in my ears. "What are you doing?"

"Shh, Etta." His voice sounded strange and different.

"What are you doing?"

"Just playing our game."

"This is not a game," I said, pushing him as hard as I could.

He rolled off the bed onto the floor and scrambled to get up. He was wearing only white cotton underwear his private part peeking out from the unbuttoned opening. It looked scary. I wanted to look away. I couldn't. I had never seen a man's private part before. He started fumbling with the buttons trying to cover him self. My stomach was churning like it was trying to crawl up my throat. I kept swallowing and swallowing and swallowing hoping to force it back where it belonged.

"I didn't mean to scare you," he whispered, "I thought you were awake."

"I don't believe you," I stuttered. My whole body was shaking and I still felt like throwing up. He didn't seem like Charlie anymore and he definitely didn't seem like my brother. "Get out," I managed to whisper.

"I'm sorry," he kept saying over and over, surprised but grateful she wasn't screaming. He opened the door and slipped out.

I jumped out of bed, closed the door and twisted the lock. I leaned against its smooth hard surface trying to control my trembling. I closed my eyes, felt tears running down my cheeks and dripping off

96

my chin. I couldn't get the image of his scary private part out of my mind. My stomach was churning again forcing me to keep swallowing.

I looked around my room, at my books scattered on the floor, at my writing pads and pencils lying neatly on my desk, at my swing chair. I stared at the framed pictures of Mama and Papa and Becca even Charlie hanging on the wall, staring like silent witnesses. I hated Charlie. He had intruded on my space. It no longer felt comfortable and familiar.

It didn't feel like my room anymore.

CHARLIE

25

Luck was with him. The hallway was empty, the house quiet. He hurried to his room and softly closed the door. He was shaking and his heart was pounding in his ears. He couldn't believe he had actually snuck into Etta's bedroom, even slipped into her bed. He could still smell her scent, feel her warmth, the softness of her skin. Why was he so obsessed with her? She was his sister, a kid, still innocent, naïve, and trusting. He was selfish and egotistical and taking advantage, which didn't bother him. That's the way he was. Besides, it usually got him what he wanted. And he wanted Etta.

Had he screwed up, gone too far? He told her it was a game, just a game between the two of them played only when on one else was around. To him it was. It was new and exciting and different, a challenge. He loved challenges, especially when he won. But what if she got tired or scared of playing? What if she told? He kept waiting for Papa to stomp into his room, beat the hell out of him and kick him out of the house. It never happened. Etta didn't tell. He was more than relieved, but her attitude toward him completely changed. She seldom smiled and talked only when Papa or Mama or Rebecca was around. He needed her to get over it. He missed her. He wanted their relationship back.

ETTA

26

I couldn't look at Charlie. Although I hated him, I missed him too. I could still feel his touch, making my stomach flip-flop and my breast tingle. I didn't want it to end. What was wrong with me? He was my brother. I definitely knew brothers and sisters were not supposed to feel this way about each other. I couldn't pretend any longer. But I didn't know how to stop my feelings.

I don't know what Charlie was thinking. He tried to act like nothing had happened, especially around Papa and Mama even Becca. I couldn't believe his cool. He started teasing me again, stopped giving me his look, acted like I was just his pesky kid sister. What was wrong with them? Couldn't they see something was different?

My feelings were making me crazy. How could I love and hate my brother at the same time? Angela popped into my mind again and again and again, but I was scared of what she would think, what she would do or whom she would tell. I thought about telling Becca but I knew she would just blame me, not Charlie. I desperately wanted to tell Mama but thought she should have known. Maybe not exactly what but that something was wrong. Weren't mamas supposed to know when things weren't right with their kids? But Mama was still Mama. Papa was still Papa. Becca was still Becca. Even Charlie was still Charlie. Only I had changed and nobody seemed to notice.

I should have told. I should have told. I should have told. It's that simple. I should have told, but what's that old saying about hindsight? That's all I've got to say about it.

I was so caught up in my own misery I hadn't noticed Mama was sick. It took Becca to bring it to my attention. She was in the kitchen baking a chicken, mashing potatoes and sautéing green beans with bacon.

"Why are you cooking?" I asked, unable to hide my surprise.

"Because I couldn't find where were you hiding," she replied in a sullen voice.

I didn't feel like arguing. I ignored her words. "Where's Mama?"

"Mama's sick."

"Sick." I thought my heart might stop.

"Yes, Etta, sick."

"Why didn't you tell me?"

"If you weren't so wrapped up in your own self, you would have known," she said, sullenness still in her voice. "It must be contagious, Charleston's been acting the same way." She sighed and rolled her eyes. "Mama's been sick since last week," she added.

"What's wrong with her?"

"I just have a cold, Etta," Mama said scuffling into the kitchen. "It's not as bad as your sister is making it sound." She took the chicken out of the oven and pricked it with a fork, its clear juices running free. "It looks delicious, Rebecca. I'll make a cook out of you yet."

Becca acted like she hadn't heard. I looked at Mama. She looked the same but she was breathing hard and fast and it sounded kind of funny. She even wobbled a little when she walked.

"What's the matter, Mama?" I asked, trying not to sound scared. I touched her arm. It felt funny too.

"It's a cold, Etta."

"You feel hot."

"I have a little fever. I'm drinking lots of fluids."

"Maybe you should see Dr. Booker." Dr. Booker was our family doctor. He had been for as long as I could remember. He was tall and skinny and stern and white, and seemed old, but his voice was quiet and calm and always made you feel like everything was going to be okay.

"Nonsense. It's just one of those pesky summer colds, sweetie," she said, coughing.

It was loud and rough sounding. I didn't believe her.

"Does Papa think you need to see Dr. Booker?"

"You know your father. He's ready to run us off to the doctor for any little thing. It's a cold, Etta. I'll get over it."

But, she didn't. Her cough got worse, so did her breathing, and her fever got hotter. Papa called Dr. Booker.

He stayed closed up in their bedroom a long time. Becca, Charlie, and I waited outside their door trying to hear. We heard only muffled voices and Mama's loud coughing. I peeked at Charlie. I hadn't paid him any attention since he had disrupted my space. His eyes were red like he wasn't getting enough sleep or was drinking too much or had been crying. His gaze met mine and he moved closer. I started to back away. He grabbed my hand and held it tight. I didn't resist. I felt my body calming, my fingers clinging to his.

"Your mother has pneumonia," Papa said trying to hide the trembles in his voice. He gathered us in the kitchen at the big round wooden table. I don't know why, but I thought Mama would have

101

preferred the dining room. Papa didn't seem like Papa. His shirt was wrinkled, he looked tired, and I thought I saw tears in his eyes.

"What's pneumonia, Papa?" I asked, although I wasn't sure I wanted to know.

"It's an inflammation, Etta, in the lungs."

"How do you get it?" I saw the annoyed look on Becca's face, but didn't care. I was scared.

"Dr. Booker said from a bacteria or a virus."

"Is that how Mama got it?" I asked, trying to understand his words.

"How would Papa know?" Becca said, "Quit asking so many questions."

"Its okay, Rebecca." Papa gave me a thin smile. "Probably."

"Is it serious?"

"Yes," he said.

"Do people die from it?"

"Yes," he repeated.

That scared us. We became mutes, holding our breaths, waiting for his next words.

"Your mother is not going to die, Etta," Papa said.

"How do you know, Papa?" I whispered, staring at him. Becca and Charlie were staring at him, too, the same question in their eyes and on their lips.

"Your mother is not going to die," Papa said again, "I won't allow it. Besides, Dr. Booker said he caught it early and the medicine will help her get well, but it will take time. All of us will have to pitch in. I'll be staying home for a few days so Charleston you will be responsible for my clients."

"Whatever you say, Papa," Charlie said.

"Rebecca and Etta will do the chores here and help me take care of Anna."

Becca and I nodded.

How do we do that? I wanted to ask Papa. I didn't. If he didn't tell me, I knew Becca would.

It was serious. Mama was really sick. She coughed and coughed and couldn't breathe. Her fever was high sometimes and her body felt like it was on fire. Other times she was trembling so bad the bed shook. Becca and I and Papa cooled her body with frequent alcohol sponge baths, changed her soaked sheets two, three, sometime four times a day, wrapped her in warm blankets to stop her chills, and forced liquids and crushed up pills down her throat. Dr. Booker stopped by every day, sometimes twice. He looked concerned but didn't let it slip into his words. I felt sorry for Mama. She mumbled out of her head and slept like she was dead. She scared me. But Papa and Becca were calm. And Charlie was a real surprise. When he got off the road, he helped with whatever chores needed to be done. He sat with Mama for hours wiping her hot face with a cool washcloth or just holding her hand talking and sharing his day.

Every night I prayed for Mama not to die.

Mama began to get better. She could talk without coughing. Her fever stayed down longer and didn't go up as high. She was awake for longer periods of time, fussed about being tied to the bed, begged to get up and go to the toilet. Little by little, her appetite improved and she no longer jabbered nonsense. When the fevers were gone and the coughing had stopped and she could breathe easy again, Dr. Booker stopped coming.

And Papa went back to work.

Although Mama was better, she was still exhausted. She took afternoon naps and that worn-out haggard look lingered in her eyes. Becca and I continued to do most of the household chores. We didn't argue, or complain, or fuss. We were too happy and relieved to have Mama almost back to being Mama. So was Papa. And Charlie.

I close my eyes and see Mama. Lord knows that was some kind of trying time. Mama was so sick and ole man death was all over that room, whispering in her ears, spinning his web, trying to claim her as his own. But Mama was strong. She put up a good fight and defied him. Mama was lucky. We were lucky. Even today, with all this modern medicine, people still die from pneumonia. I couldn't have lived if Mama had died. I suspect none of us could. I'm exaggerating, of course, but this I know is true, our lives wouldn't have been the same.

CHARLIE

28

Mama's sickness scared Charlie. Mama seemed resilient, always there whenever they needed her. Papa was head of household but Charlie suspected Mama was the one that kept it all together. He couldn't imagine their lives without her. So, at the end of his days on the road, he stayed close, clinging to her hand, sharing his day and praying for her recovery.

He tried to put on a mask, be strong so Papa wouldn't see how weak and scared he was. He was the oldest and the only son. He knew he was expected to be a man, to be dependable. And he was. Except in his room behind closed doors when he fell apart crying into his pillows. What if Mama died?

He knew they were all scared - Rebecca, Etta, even Papa. All of them were wearing the mask of toughness. They didn't want each other to know their true feelings. He was missing Etta, missing her closeness, wished they could comfort each other, but she was ignoring him. They were no longer connected. Still, when he reached out to her, she responded, but it wasn't the same. It was only temporary. He had only himself to blame.

At least his prayers were answered. Mama didn't die.

ETTA

29

Papa was more protective of Mama after her sickness. He came home early most evenings, worked only half days on Saturdays, stopped working all together on Sundays, and continued to put more of his workload on Charlie. The thought of Mama dying had scared him, too, I guess. And Mama seemed different. The pneumonia had been hard on her, leaving her weak and worn-out. Exhausted. She sometimes leaned against a kitchen counter or slipped onto a chair, and there was a hint of sadness in her eyes making me still scared. What if she got it again?

"Is that possible, Papa?"

"I suppose anything's possible, Etta, but Dr. Booker took good care of your mother. He says her lungs are clear and he's keeping her on medicine and thanks to you and Rebecca, she's getting plenty of rest. I'm proud of both of you and Charleston. You've all been a big help. Your mother just needs time that's all. She's going to be fine."

I wanted to believe Papa, but I kept watching Mama. I kept waiting for her to start coughing or breathing funny or her skin to feel hot. I was always asking her how she felt. It worried me so much I made the mistake of mentioning it to Becca. She was no help, of course.

"Quit being dramatic, Etta. Papa's right. Mama's going to be fine. And stop asking her how she feels."

I had to give it to Becca, though. She was trying to be nice and even tried to stop whining. It didn't always work but at least she was trying.

I mentioned it to Charlie, too. Charlie and I were acting like sister and brother, again. We had agreed to forget about all that past stuff. Mama's sickness, the idea she might die, had scared all of us. We couldn't imagine life without Mama.

She was supposed to be better, but I worried because she still seemed different. I said that to Charlie.

"Different how?" he asked.

"I don't know, Charlie, she's just different."

"You need to be more specific, Etta."

I sighed and stared at him. He was different too but I didn't say that. "She's more quiet," I said.

"Mama was never loud."

"Quiet's not the right word. She always seems pooped."

"She's just getting over pneumonia, remember. Her body is still healing. Wait a few weeks." He sounded like Papa.

"You're not afraid she'll never get better?" I asked, staring at him.

"No," he said, like he believed it. He stared back and I saw that look forming in his eyes.

"We agreed," I said, ignoring it.

I stopped worrying about Mama. She did get better just like Papa, Charlie, and Becca had said. She was back to doing most of the cooking and other household chores. She was even pretty again, looked like Mama. She laughed, hummed, and danced to the music on the radio like Mama, argued with Papa, fussed at Charlie, Becca, and me, like Mama. Mama was back.

The clock was ticking on summer. Tiny subtle hints that it was moving into fall began to appear. The days were a mite - just a mite - shorter, and night started hanging around a tiny bit longer. Even the sun seemed less hot and the scary violent weather didn't come as often.

I had mixed feelings about fall. I loved the warm days with their slight chill and the trees beginning to change their outlandish colors. But fall seemed to bring sadness with it like, Mama's sickness. It didn't last, but it was there at the beginning, making me sad too. I knew this year it was going to be worse. Becca would be leaving. She was going less than a hundred miles away, which meant she would probably be home most weekends and holidays. And I could go along when Papa and Mama went to visit, but she would still be gone, making my days a little lonelier and my list of chores longer. I couldn't believe I was going to miss Becca.

Charlie was a whole different story. I wanted to think his leaving would be a relief. At least it would put a stop to this thing that had been going on between us. But to be honest, II was going to miss Charlie more than I was going to miss Becca. I had gotten too involved with Charlie.

ETTA

30

Even though summer was definitely coming to an end, the days stayed hot and sticky and unbearable with no breeze. It was that kind of Saturday when Charlie suggested going on a picnic. Papa had let Charlie have the car since he and Mama would be tied-up all day. Our church had gotten the nod to host the annual convention, a pretty big event attended by people from all over. To accommodate everybody, it was usually held in a city or a good size town where hotels and restaurants that catered to colored people were available. The smaller churches, ours included, complained, felt left out and decided to challenge the powers that be. They started putting in their own bids every year. That our church was chosen was no small feat. The members were pleasantly shocked and probably had some regrets since they would be responsible for housing the delegates and providing most of the meals. No one complained, at least not out loud. They just gave thanks and got to work. And it was work. The entire congregation was busy all winter and spring sprucing up the church, painting, cleaning, and tending the lawns. They scrubbed down the kitchen, cleaned the stoves, the ovens, and restocked the shelves. The women ironed tablecloths, washed china, glasses, and silverware, planned menus, and made out schedules. Everybody wanted to make a good impression. Everything had to be perfect, especially since folks were still grumbling and complaining about the sorry state of the last convention. Our small band of members was determined to show they could do it right. I wanted Mama to sign up to house people, cause that sounded kind of fun and we had the room, but she didn't. I guess she figured she would be too busy with Charlie and Becca leaving soon after. It turned out to be a good decision, since she had gotten pneumonia.

31

The convention was finally here and it was as busy and chaotic as everybody expected. Saturday was one of the biggest days. Charlie had dropped Papa, Mama, and Becca off early. Charlie and I were surprised Becca even wanted to go, but she had become involved with some of the young people, mostly college students. She tried to include Charlie, but being his egotistical self, he had no interest.

"Let's go on a picnic," he said, when he got back.

"A picnic?"

"Yes, Etta, a picnic."

"Where?"

"I don't know. We can drive until we find a place."

"Can I ask Mavis or Angela?"

"Ask whoever you want."

Unfortunately, Mavis had something planned and Angela was stuck babysitting, since her mama and papa were also tied up at the convention. That meant it would be Charlie and me. I wasn't sure I wanted to be alone with Charlie, but it was too hot to read, and I wasn't in the mood for writing. If I didn't go, I'd be home alone bored and restless and wishing I had.

"Hmm, a picnic," I said, again, stalling.

"Just say yes or no, okay." There was annoyance in his voice.

"What are we going to eat?"

"Mama left food. I can pack it up and bring it with us."

I had to admit a picnic sounded like fun and the day was perfect.

Charlie was driving fast, concentrating on the road. His window was down, dark glasses covered his eyes and a toothpick was wedged between his lips. He was taking Route Six, a narrow, curvy road that went away from town. Sunshine poured through the windshield, baking our bodies. The smell of lilacs and honeysuckle filled the air and the wide-open fields on the sides of the road were covered with delicate dandelion blossoms twitching in a wave of yellow.

"Slow down, Charlie."

He glanced at me and grinned. "I'm not going that fast."

"Yeah, you are," I said, shading my eyes with the back of my hand trying to block out the sun.

"Fast is what makes it fun."

"Papa's rule was not to go beyond the speed limit, remember?"

"I think you're scared."

"Okay, I'm scared."

He eased his foot off the gas. "Better?"

"I thought this was supposed to be a nice, easy outing?"

"It is."

"It sure doesn't feel like it. Why are you in such a hurry anyhow?"

"It's the car, Etta, it was made for going fast."

"Tell that to Papa."

He laughed. "I'm not stupid."

We rode in silence. The sun was making a mockery of the breeze coming from the open windows and the heat was making me restless. I pulled down the sun visor and wished I had dark glasses too.

"Where does this road go?"

"There's a little park about 5-10 miles down the way."

"Charlie, you lied, you knew exactly where we were going."

"No, I didn't."

He must have felt me staring.

He glanced at me. "Honest," he said.

"I don't believe you."

"Etta, I just remembered."

"How did you even know there was a park out here?"

"Papa and I discovered it coming back from Hogan. That's what I like about going with Papa. I see places and things I didn't know existed. It's kind of cool."

"I'm surprised you're still doing it. Becca and I figured you just went so you could learn how to drive. We thought you'd quit once you did."

"Why do you and Rebecca always think I have an ulterior motive?"

"Confess, Charlie, you know we were right."

He laughed again. "It worked. I'm just surprised I like it."

"We all are, especially Papa. I think he's hoping you'll follow in his footsteps."

"Are you kidding? I've been honest with Papa about that possibility."

"He can still hope. Do you like college?"

"Love it. I've met all kinds of students and I'm my own boss and its fun and exciting and . . ."

"Becca was right. That's really why you didn't come home for two years."

"Do you blame me?"

"I wonder if Becca will like it."

"I don't know. Rebecca's kind of private."

"Well, I can't wait," I said, squirming around on the hot seat.

"You'll like it, Etta. You're a lot like me."

"No I'm not, but I think I'll like it too."

Charlie took his foot off the gas, almost bringing the car to a stop, and turned into a skinny dirt packed road that hardly seemed wide enough for a car. He drove at a snail's pace, the tires crunching on the worn down uneven gravel, making the car bump up and down. A rough wooden sign with the faded words, Jones Park, was leaning precariously on one side of the road.

"How did you and Papa ever find this place?" I asked, feeling like we were in the middle of nowhere.

"Papa thought it was just a turn around," he said, keeping his eyes straight ahead. "The park surprised us."

The dirt path finally ended at a small empty cracked parking lot. Charlie turned off the engine and got out of the car. "You have to walk a little ways."

I pushed my door open wide with my foot and wriggled out. It felt good to stretch and move around.

"Come on slow poke."

"Shouldn't we get the stuff out of the trunk?"

"I'll come back for it. I want you to see the park."

ETTA

32

I followed him down a narrow stone path shaded by trees. It was cool and I could feel a breeze, a welcome relief from the sun. Beyond the trees was a wide open space, the grass still green and lush even this late in summer. There were a few wooden tables with benches, a small playground with four swings, a slide and a tiny colorful merry-go-round. There was even a paved fenced in tennis court with a taut net.

"This is nice."

"I knew you'd like it."

"It's quiet and peaceful. Where is everybody?"

"Give them time. Pick out a spot while I get the stuff."

"Do you need help?"

"I can manage."

The park was small, seemed more like a field. I could see most of it from where I was standing. I had to admit I was glad I came. I wandered over to a clump of trees on the fringe of the playground. It was shady but sunlight still filtered through the tree branches. A perfect spot at least until kids showed up. Charlie was walking across the grass, carrying Papa's big round thermos and Mama's picnic basket, a blanket thrown over one shoulder.

"What do you think?" I asked, taking the basket.

"Perfect." He put down the thermos and spread Mama's old blanket over the grass, straightening out the edges. I forgot he was a neat freak. He plopped down on his knees, leaning back on his heels, took a cigarette out of his pocket and lit it with his lighter.

"Sit," he said, patting a spot next to him.

I sat the basket on the grass and eased down feeling the blades poking through the worn blanket against my skin. Charlie stretched out on his back, crossed his legs and folded one arm under his head. He was staring at the cloudless sky, his cigarette dangling between his lips. I unhooked the basket and opened the lid.

"You're hungry already?" he asked, not stirring.

"Just curious." I poked around inside. There were sandwiches wrapped in wax paper, tomatoes, carrots, radishes in paper sacks, several bright red apples, and a small bag of cookies. Paper plates, cups, spoons, knives and forks were stuffed down the sides.

"What's in the thermos?"

"Iced tea."

"I'm impressed. You thought of everything."

He laughed, turned on his side toward me and snuffed his cigarette out in the grass.

I lay back on the blanket, closed my eyes and felt the sun on my face and arms through the flimsy cotton material of my blouse. I could sense Charlie squirming beside me. I smelled his soap, his shaving cream and the strong trace of tobacco clinging to his skin. My body tensed and that funny good feeling began to stir in the pit of my stomach and spread down between my legs. I felt his fingers brush my cheeks, linger at my lips, creep slowly down my neck.

"I've changed my mind," I said, sitting up and moving away. "I am hungry." I scooted to the picnic basket, took out a sandwich, pulled away the wrapping exposing a thick slice of meatloaf between whole wheat bread.

"Want one?" I asked, taking a bite.

He shook his head.

I chewed and swallowed and took another bite, tasted nothing, hoped it wouldn't come back up. His silence was making me nervous. "Penny for your thoughts."

"I'm going to miss you," he said.

I shook my head. "You'll be too busy liking college again." I tried to laugh away his words.

"Will you miss me?"

"Charlie, what a silly question, of course, we'll miss you. Maybe not Becca so much, but Papa and Mama . . ."

"Will you?"

Shut up I wanted to yell.

"Etta?"

"What?"

"Will you . . ."

"Why do you keep asking?" I interrupted, unable to keep the meanness out of my voice.

"Because we've had this special something between us. Aren't you going to miss that?"

He was staring at me.

"Yes," I said, "yes, yes, yes, but I'm glad you're going. These feelings are wrong."

"Does this feel wrong," he asked, moving closer, running his fingers up and down my bare arm."

His touch felt different. I didn't have the words to describe it, but it had never felt like this before. My young mind and virgin body didn't know what to make of it, but I liked it, liked its softness, gentleness, the way it made my stomach flutter and parts of my body tingle. It scared me though. So I moved away, trying to create space between us. I didn't recognize the look in his eyes, either, scaring me even more. I started shivering, felt goose bumps popping out on my skin and felt the sandwich slip out of my hand.

"Or this?" kissing me on the mouth, "or this?" slipping his tongue between my lips.

I was squirming and breathing funny. Stop, please stop, was running through my head, but my body wasn't listening, just responding to his touch. Everything seemed to be happening in slow motion. His hands were opening my blouse and fingering my nipples. He slipped one breast out of my flimsy brassier, sucked gently. I couldn't breathe; felt that funny cramping in my stomach, then realized he was getting on top of me, pressing his body close. I felt his private part, big and hard against my belly. My mind was shouting stop but my body wasn't listening. I tried to push him off, but it felt like we were glued together. He was unzipping his pants, pulling up my skirt and sliding down my underpants. He started pushing his private part into the opening between my legs. It didn't go. He pushed harder, hurting me, until it was in. I whimpered wanting to scream. He eased out, a little, slipped it back in, started moving in and out, in and out, catching me up in his rhythm. My body seemed out of control like some "thing" had taken it over, possessed it, leaving me helpless and at its mercy.

He collapsed on top of me. I couldn't breathe. I thought I was dying. Frantically, I started pushing and shoving, trying to get free. He rolled off, breathing loud. I lay still, trying to stop the confused thoughts swimming in my head. I couldn't move, refused to think, and couldn't believe what he had done. My stomach cramped, my thighs hurt and there was sticky wetness between my legs. I smelled his stench, turned on my side and threw up.

I was afraid to look around. We were in a public place. What if someone saw us? Oh God this was bad, real bad. I started to cry.

"Shh, Etta," he was saying. "It's going to be okay."

"No it's not," I screamed. "It's never going to be okay again."

CHARLIE

33

Charlie knew she was right, but he had little remorse. Summer was almost over and college was looming. It was time to go. He had let things go way too far and the longer he stayed, the worse it would get. He seemed unable to control his thoughts, feelings and actions toward Etta. He was relieved he was leaving. Getting away was exactly what he needed. It was the only way to end it and it needed to end. She was his sister. He couldn't change that. Did she really excite him that much or had it just been a whim, a way to pass the summer?

Whatever it had been, he would never share it. It was their secret, his having sex with his sister the summer she turned fifteen. He knew it was wrong, sick even, and if she ever told, he was in big trouble. He knew Papa would kill him.

ETTA

34

Charlie's words echo in my head as I click off the machine. Tears well in my eyes and I feel slightly dizzy. Images of him fill my head: his rolled up cotton pants, bare feet, fuzzy sandy hair, crooked smile and brash, know-it-all attitude. I even smell traces of the pungent tobacco odor that clung to his skin and seeped through his pores. I search the recorder's erase button needing to wipe out my words. I keep fiddling with the machine trying to figure out which button will make them disappear, stuff them back into the recesses of my memories or nightmares where they have been all these years. I mumble a curse and put on my glasses. This technical mess is confusing. I finally push pause. The machine goes silent but my words are still trapped inside. The images linger. My heart hurts or maybe it's my soul. I take a deep breath hoping to ease the pain and stop the trembling.

The room is quiet; the air around me so still it seems my heart has stopped. I only know it's beating because I can hear it pounding in my ears. Nothing moves, nothing, not even the flimsy lace curtains covering the open windows billowing from the light breeze. My body seems paralyzed and my mind transfixed. I shake my limbs and my head trying to return them to the present. Lord only knows why I agreed to this. It's been months, three long months, since I started. It was winter then. Temperatures stayed below freezing, snow covered the ground and ice sickles, thick as young tree roots, hung from the eaves. Now spring is just around the corner with gentle breezes and warm snow-melting days. I've spent hours, sometimes whole days, even nights talking about my past. My words lie like stones on my chest and my mind is disrupted, but the tape is full. I can finally stop my words, at least temporarily, and Lord knows, I want to, especially after . . . .

I wanted to leave it out, just skip over it like it never happened, like I've tried to do for longer than I can remember. That's why it's taken so long. My mind simply refused to go there; back to all that pain and misery, to that place and time that ruined my life. I had to keep nudging it, memory by painful memory. It's been decades, but talking about it still makes me feel dirty, and guilty, and ashamed. I've tried so hard to bury it but telling is bringing it all back. It's in my head again, that glorious late summer day, the beautiful little park, the feel of the sun on my face, and the horror that was Charlie. How in the world will I ever get it back in its burial place?

Why I am doing it now? Now when anybody who would have mattered is dead and buried except Becca. Becca, whose mind is often so lost and confused she might as well be dead. And me?

Francesca.

Smart, aggressive, pretty, Francesca, the daughter of my old friend, Angela. Francesca practically grew up in my house. We baked cookies, read books, popped corn on cold wintery nights and had long heated discussions. She called me Auntie, and I treated her like the daughter I never had. She was bright and inquisitive, fascinated with family histories and bloodlines, always suspicious of undocumented truths. She got a degree in genealogy and traced her family's history back to its African roots.

My long life fascinates Francesca. She wears me out with questions, insists I have stories, experiences, maybe even secrets. She nags me, afraid they'll get lost in my deteriorating memory, fills my eighty-six year old head with all that "getting if off your chest nonsense;" that "give you some peace of mind" kind of mess.

"What makes you think I don't already have peace of mind, that I even have something to tell?" I fuss.

"You've lived a long life, Auntie. You must have things you've kept to yourself."

"There ain't no crime in that, child."

"I thought you agreed it's important to be honest about history," she argues, "that you can't change the past to make it pretty or delete the parts that are unpleasant?"

"I do, but this is me, Francesca, Etta Mae Netter. This is my personal stuff you wanting to meddle in. I'm not sure I'm willing to do that."

"So, I'm right."

"Is that what I said?"

"No, Ma'am," she mumbles.

She sounds so pitiful I pat her hand and give her a smile. "Let me think on it."

I give it lots of thought. In fact, it stays on my mind. Lord knows I don't want to stir up all that ugly mess. It's been more than seventy years. Sometimes it seems that long, even longer. Sometimes I hardly think about it. Sometimes it seems like last year or last month or yesterday, but never like never. It just won't let me go completely.

Seventy-one years.

The longer I ponder, the more I know she's right. Becca warns me to keep quiet. She argues that no good can come from running off at the mouth.

I should have listened to Becca.

I wait a while before contacting Francesca. She's anxious to pick up the tape. She's been calling and the few times she's visited, she's mentioned it. But I want to hate Francesca. I want to change my mind and lie, tell her I erased it, so I can keep that part of my past secret. It takes every ounce of my will power to keep me from doing just that, but, I am not a liar, and not about to start at this age. Besides, she'll know I'm lying. I'm not educated enough about the workings of this terrible little machine. I do wonder what Francesca will think when she listens to my words. How will she react? I suspect this is not what she's expecting to hear. It will probably catch her off guard. Will she be shocked, disgusted, think me some kind of fool? Will she understand how I could have been so naïve? Will she respect me still?

So be it. I gave the child my word, promised to tell my history, and my word is my bond. Even though it still hurts and she'll know the truth, I'm committed. What was it she said about history? Something about not changing it to make it pretty, or deleting parts that are unpleasant? God sure made you wise, Francesca.

I call and hear the excitement in her voice. She brings a new tape, anxious to listen to the filled-up one. She gives me a big hug and thanks me for my willingness to share. Silly old me to think I could ever hate Francesca. She's such a loving appreciative youngster.

But, unlike her, I'm in no hurry. I put the fresh tape on the top shelf of my bookcase. I cannot start the telling again so soon. My mind and memories are still hung up, lost in the past. I'm sleeping poorly and Charlie, Papa, and Mama, even Malcolm, are popping up in my dreams, my nightmares.

ETTA

35

I need to talk to Becca. We are the only two left, and after all these years, we are not close, not like I think sisters should be. But then we never were. Oh, we talk, argue mostly, over the phone, and see each other at one place or another every now and again. But there's little warmth in our meetings. She long ago damned me to hell for ruining our family. She still does.

We both live in the same small Iowa town, it's gotten a little bigger but hasn't changed a whole lot. I even live in the house we grew up in, with the wrap-around front porch I still love. Becca left the town for the city shortly after she graduated college. When she returned, she wanted no part of living in our house. She said it held too many unpleasant thoughts and moved into a senior complex on Main Street. She keeps saying I should do the same. It's nice, I'll admit that, but I remember when Coloreds couldn't do nothin on Main Street except clean rich white women's houses. She says I'm being ridiculous that was a long time ago. Maybe I am, but I prefer living in a place I was always welcomed. And to be honest, l don't fancy living that close to Becca or being around just seniors all day every day. I don't need that constant reminder that I'm one of them. We do stay in touch though.

Sadly, as she's gotten older, her mind has, too, slipping from alertness into forgetfulness and confusion. For some reason, I feel guilty about that. I miss her. I wish I could help her, wish I could replace all those senile plaques scattered through out her brain with coherent thoughts and words and memories. I never thought I'd long for the whiny, egotistical Becca of our youth, but I do. These days,

I'm never sure how she'll be, coherent, her mind in the present, or off in some strange world of its own. But I need to talk to her. I take the chance and call.

"Becca, its Etta."

"Why do you always assume I won't recognize your voice?"

Cause some days you don't, I want to remind her.

"You know that's just my way of connecting," I say, glad she seems alert and sounds like Becca.

"So, who died?" she asks, really sounding like her old sarcastic self.

I chuckle. "Nobody."

"Then, why are you calling?"

"Do I need a reason? Can't I just want to talk, to hear your voice?"

"You must be feeling the need to punish yourself again."

Even with her confusion, she can still read my thoughts.

"I told you not to let that gal talk you into all that nonsense. Didn't I tell you?"

"Yes, Becca, you told me."

"You should have listened, you know. Now, she's got you so upset you can't remember your manners. You didn't even ask how I was doing."

"Sorry," I mumble, feeling like a youngster. "How are you?"

"Fine now that you ask," she grumbles. "You're out of sorts because of those tapes."

"I can't argue with that."

"Why do you only listen to your big sister after shit happens?"

I ignore her words. As I said, she blames me for ruining our lives. Even after all these years, she still blames me. And I know neither of us will live long enough to change that, so I ignore her words.

125

"You know Mama and Papa are going to be mad at you, Etta, for telling our family secrets," she drones on, slight anger now mixed in with her sarcasm.

"No, they wouldn't, Becca. I think they would want me to have some peace of mind. Besides, they're dead, remember, long time dead."

"Why do you keep saying that, Etta? You know that's not so. I spose you're going to tell me Charleston's dead too?"

"You know yes."

"And Malcolm?"

"Him too," I whisper.

I hear her soft cries. "Why can't I ever remember that?" She breaks our connection.

I put the receiver back on the hook, wanting to cry too, and wonder if she's right. Would Papa and Mama be upset? No, I know that in my heart, truly I do, Charlie maybe, but who cares about Charlie? Charlie stopped counting long ago. I feel the familiar sadness creeping into my soul. Talking to Becca always depresses me. Why can't I ever remember that?

I change my mind. I want to finish this telling, get it off my chest and out of my head. I want to put the past back in the past and get on with the short time of living I suspect I have left. Continuing is going to be difficult, but maybe just maybe; when it's over and done, and there's no more to tell, my mind will finally be at peace. I take the tape off the shelf and put it in the machine.

PART TWO

ETTA
36

I didn't tell Mama and Papa what happened that hot afternoon in the small park in the middle of nowhere. Charlie decided it would be our secret. I went along because I was scared and ashamed and didn't know what else to do. Besides, what was done was done and I couldn't change it. We both knew it was his fault, but had I tried hard enough to stop him? Maybe it was my fault too. What would Papa and Mama say or do or think of me? Could smart-ass Charlie make me the scapegoat and convince them I had egged him on? Would Papa take up for Charlie as usual? I cried all the way home. My eyes were red and puffy and just thinking about it made me want to throw up. *It didn't happen. It didn't happen*, kept running through my mind.

Guilt was putting strange thoughts in my head. Was Becca giving me funny looks like it was written all over my face? Was Mama suspicious? Did she know something wasn't right but was too busy getting things together for Charlie's and Becca's leaving to bring it up?

"Be patient with me, Etta," I thought I heard her saying, "when these two are out of my hair, it'll be your turn."

I can wait, Mama, I can wait.

Charlie left first. We all went to the train station to see him off. I wanted to stay home but couldn't think of a good enough excuse. Mama packed him a lunch, and Papa slipped a few extra dollars into his suit pocket. We all waited awkwardly on the platform for the train to ease into the station.

"I'm going to miss you, Son," Papa said, giving him a hug. "You were a good assistant. Now, I'll have to get used to doing everything myself, again."

"We're all going to miss you, Charleston," Mama said, wiping at her tears.

"Speak for yourself, Mama," Becca grumbled.

Amen to that.

"You know you're going to miss me, Rebecca," Charlie said, grinning.

"No I'm not Charleston; I'll be busy getting used to college."

"That's right," he said, "I forgot you'll be off to college too. You'll like it."

"Says who?"

"Says me, Rebecca. Trust me."

Becca didn't respond, just rolled her eyes.

"And what about you, Etta, are you going to miss me?"

"Son, you won't be gone that long," Papa said, laughing. "The holidays are right around the corner."

"Papa's right," I said. "You won't be gone that long."

"It might be longer than you think."

I saw that look in his eyes. What did he mean? What did he know that I didn't? Would he even be coming home for the holidays?

He gave me a hug and whispered in my ear, "Remember, it's our secret."

You don't have to remind me, I wanted to scream, suddenly relieved and glad the train was taking him away. Maybe now I could get back to being me.

I watched him hug Papa and Mama and Becca again, give me one last look, a bold crooked smile on his lips, watched him standing on the train steps, waving as it pulled out of the station, watched until the train was just a speck down the tracks. It felt like part of my heart was leaving. I could smell his tobacco; feel his touch and that funny-good feeling in the pit of my stomach. I wanted to cry.

132

"Yeah, I'll miss you, Charlie," I whispered, struggling to hide my tears.

A week later, Papa and Mama loaded up the car and drove Becca to college. I went along for the ride. Becca was nervous, trying hard not to show it, but I could feel her tension.

"Relax, Becca, being away from home is going to be fun."

"And how would you know, Etta? Have you been away from home?"

I shook my head. "Charlie has and he likes it."

"I'm not Charleston."

The boarding house where Becca would be living was huge, three stories with lots of windows, a big shady yard and stone steps leading to a grand front porch. The housemother greeted us warmly and showed Becca to her room. It was clean and airy, homey and filled with light. It was kind of small, cause Becca didn't want a roommate, but nice. Mama and Papa were relieved, only Becca didn't seem impressed, but that was just Becca. Besides she was still upset colored students couldn't stay in the dorms even though she knew that when she applied.

We unloaded her belongings and lugged them up to her room. Mama started fiddling with things until Papa suggested going to eat before driving home. No one seemed hungry but we went anyway. I guess Papa was trying to delay our leaving. He finally drove back to the elegant old house. Becca didn't want us to come up to her room, so Papa let her out in front, left her standing small and alone on the curb. I stared out the car's back window as he drove away waving and watching her get smaller and smaller not even trying to hide my tears.

With Becca and Charlie gone, I couldn't wait for school to start. School would be my saving grace. It would keep me busy with studies, help keep my mind off Charlie, not miss Becca so much, and get me reconnected with Mavis and Angela. Yeah, school was going to be my Savior.

It was for a while. I had a heavy schedule and hooking up with Angela and Mavis kept all of us busy. Angela was trying out for the girls' basketball team and the glee club, and Mavis for the cheerleading squad. I wasn't surprised about Angela. She was athletic and musical. Both would be a shoo-in. But Mavis as a cheerleader was more than I could imagine. She didn't fit the image. She was athletic, too, had the blonde hair and right colored eyes, but she was chubby and kind of shy, didn't have that cheery girlie thing going, wasn't part of the uptown crowd, and they were the ones that got picked. The judges would probably see her as unacceptable. I tried to talk her out of it, not wanting her to get her feelings hurt, but she was determined. Angela and I went to the tryouts to support her. She was good, which didn't surprise us. Maybe they would pick her. They didn't. She was devastated. We kept saying it was them not her. She had been good, really, really good, but she still moped around for weeks. When Angela suggested she try out for the basketball team, she did, made it, and slowly got back to being Mavis. Angela even nagged me about trying out. To shut her up, I did. I didn't make it. I had not one athletic bone in my whole body. Convinced, Angela dropped it.

The last thing I expected was a letter from Charlie so when it arrived I couldn't believe it.

"Why would Charlie be writing me?" I asked, taking the sealed white envelope from Mama.

"Why not, he's you're brother."

"But, he's never written me before."

"You two seemed to have gotten close doing the summer. Maybe he's missing you."

"Charlie?"

Mama laughed. "Well, I think it's nice, Etta. Siblings should communicate and stay in touch with each other. You'll probably hear from Rebecca, too."

"Becca write me a letter, I doubt it."

I went to my room, closed the door, sat at my desk and stared at the envelope. Charlie's name and address were typed neatly in the upper left corner. My name and address were typed just as neatly in the exact middle. I didn't know he could type. I was impressed. I opened it carefully, pulled out a folded single sheet of plain white paper and spread it on the desk, afraid of what he had said. It was short, not typed, making his handwritten words look huge.

Etta, you have to believe I didn't mean to hurt you. But I can't say I'm sorry. It was . . . special. I also want to remind you what happened between us is our secret, just you and me, okay. Don't hate me too much.

Charleston (Charlie)

P.S. Hide this from Mama and Papa and Rebecca.

I read the letter over and over trying to control my trembling and fighting the images that kept wanting to pop up in my mind. I knew I should hate him, and sometimes I did, but did he really think I would tell? Did he think me that stupid? I gave up and hid his letter like he ordered, in my underwear drawer. And when Mama asked what he said, I lied.

I should have told her right then and there, just blurted it out in all its ugliness. It seemed like perfect timing. I didn't. I was still ashamed and couldn't stand the thought of hurting Mama making her sad and disappointed. Every time I thought about what Charlie had done, I got scared, sick to my stomach, and kept trying to convince

135

myself it hadn't happened. But if I told, maybe Mama could ease my fears and make it all better like she did when I was sick or worried or just feeling bad. This was different. This was serious. I had done something terribly wrong. What would she think of me? What would Becca? And then there was Papa. I decided I couldn't tell. Besides, it had only happened once, Charlie was gone and it would never happen again. So, why did I need to tell? I managed to convince myself Charlie was right. It was our secret. Unfortunately, I would learn secrets don't always stay secret.

ETTA

37

My monthly bleeding had started at the end of my thirteenth year and even though Mama had told me about it, it was still scary and messy. My stomach felt sick and hurt, a lot, and I could hardly move, stayed in bed folded up like a baby. Luckily, it was a hit and miss kind of thing. I could go months without any trace of it, but what I wanted was for it to go away forever.

"It's just a part of becoming a woman, Etta," Mama always reminded me.

"But I'm only thirteen."

"I know, Sweetie, but you'll get used to it."

I knew I wouldn't and was glad when it didn't show up, but I hadn't had any bleeding since that awful day in the park. This time it's not showing up was scaring me. As much as I tried to forget, even deny, what Charlie had done, it was never far from my mind, popping in and out of my thoughts when I least expected it. Could I get pregnant from the first time? I wanted to stop by the library and look in that Gray's Anatomy book, for what I wasn't sure, signs of pregnancy, maybe? I also wanted to tell Mama, needed to tell Mama, needed her reassurance that I was okay. I did neither. I was too scared.

Sleepiness was the first thing that got my attention. I was sleepy all the time. I struggled to stay awake in class and was pooped by the end of the day. I went to bed early, slept all night and still didn't want to get up in the morning.

Mama started noticing.

"You're doing a lot of sleeping lately, Etta. Aren't you feeling well?"

"I feel fine Mama."

"I haven't seen you writing or heard you practicing the piano. That's not like you."

"It's school," I lied. "I have a heavy schedule."

"Oh sweetie, you have plenty of time to take all your requirements. Maybe you should think about dropping a class or two and give yourself more free time."

"I want to get them out of the way, Mama."

"Why are you in such a rush?"

"So I can take subjects I like."

"Well, don't wear yourself out," she said, laughing and kissing me on the forehead.

I felt my tears and again wanted to tell her but managed to blink them away. I gave her a weak smile instead.

Mavis was noticing too. "Are you okay?"

"Why?"

"I don't know. You seem to be dragging lately."

I laughed. "Maybe because you and Angela wear me out supporting all your after school activities."

"You don't have to come, you know."

"Yeah. I do."

"Why?"

"Because I'm your friend and that's what friends do."

"Not if it's making you sick."

"I'm not sick." And I wasn't. I was just worn out tired.

One morning I woke up with a queasy feeling in my stomach, hardly made it to the toilet before throwing up. That surprised me. I

138

never threw up. My stomach felt unsettled most of the day. I didn't throw up again, just felt like I was going to. And as much as I hated throwing up, I hated feeling like I was going to even more. That's what I got for gorging on Mama's beans and rice, I thought, except it didn't go away. Everyday, all day, I had that funny sick feeling and didn't want to eat. I sometimes felt dizzy too, and my clothes were beginning to feel kind of loose.

I finally forced myself to go to the library. I went after school on a day Angela and Mavis were at practice. I got the big book off the shelf and carried it to an empty back table. It seemed heavier than I remembered and more complicated. I couldn't find what I was looking for and I knew how to spell pregnancy. I went back to the shelf, started looking at other books. And there, right in front of my eyes, was another big one claiming to be *The Complete Book on Pregnancy*. I lugged it to the table and found what I was looking for. I stared at the words, forcing myself to read them, confirming my fears. I started trembling so hard I thought I would fall. My skin felt cold and sweaty and my stomach felt like it was crawling up my throat. I pulled out a chair, plopped down and started taking deep breaths trying to keep from crying out loud. The library was almost empty but I needed to leave. I closed the book, left it on the table with the other one, and walked away. Then, I remembered my school bag, thought about leaving it too. I went back, snatched it off the back of the chair, and managed to walk up the aisle again and out the library's double doors. Now I had to tell Mama. And she would have to tell Papa. Everybody would know - Becca, Mavis, Angela, Minister Ralph, and the church congregation, Dr. Booker, our whole little town . . . and Charlie. The thought overwhelmed me. My heart was beating in my ears, making me dizzier. I was crying and trembling and wondering how I was going to tell. I wanted to die.

I started living in a nightmare. I couldn't eat, couldn't sleep, and felt like crying all the time. My stomach felt queasy, like I was always on the verge of throwing up. When I tried to swallow, my throat felt tight, like I might choke. And every time I closed my eyes, I saw Charlie's scary private part. I didn't want to go to school, afraid my teachers would notice something was wrong. I stopped hanging out with Mavis and Angela, and stayed in my room as much as possible, using homework as my excuse. I kept staring at my body in my bedside mirror, turning from side to side, trying to see if it was changing. I was still skinny, my stomach was still flat, but my breasts were starting to feel different, and my body was beginning to feel unfamiliar, sick and tired and bloated like I had eaten too much of Mama's cooking, not at all like my usual fifteen-year old body. I had to tell.

I started practicing what I was going to say, and how I was going to say it. As hard as I tried, I could never get the words right, could never say them without crying. For some reason, Becca kept floating around in my mind. We weren't close, but I liked her and didn't want her to think badly of me. Then there was Charlie. It was his fault, I knew that, but I kept thinking it was mine too. I wondered if he already knew or suspected. I hadn't answered his letter and hadn't heard from him again. What would happen to Charlie when I told? I kept putting if off till Mama beat me to it.

"Is there something you want to tell me?"

We were in my bedroom. She still came in to say goodnight and tuck me under the covers, even though we both knew I was too old, and Papa teased her about treating me like a baby, but she still did, and I still liked it. It was our special time together.

"Etta."

I started fidgeting, almost lied and said no. It wasn't the right time. I hadn't yet gotten my words together, but tears started dripping down my cheeks.

"Tell me," she said, easing down on the bed. She put her arm around my shoulders and wiped at my tears.

"I can't."

"Yes, you can, sweetie."

"No I can't, Mama. It's too awful."

"Nothing is ever as bad as you think. You can tell me anything, remember?"

I shuddered and cried harder.

"Anything, Etta."

Why was this turning out to be so hard? Wasn't this exactly what I wanted? I took a deep breath and blurted it out, Charlie's suggestion of going on a picnic. The pretty little park no bigger than a field. Charlie and I lying on a blanket under a shade tree, his fondling, kissing, laying his body on top of mine and pushing his private part into me. It sounded bad, as bad as it had been. I was crying, hard, my words sounded like mumble jumble.

Mama was quiet, her arm squeezing me so tight it hurt. I wanted her to say something, anything. Her silence was making me feel guilty and dirty and ashamed all over again. I was shaking even though the room was warm and cozy. I wanted to look at her, but didn't want to see the hurt and disappointment I knew had to be in her eyes. I couldn't imagine what she was thinking.

"I'm sorry, I'm sorry, I'm sorry," I kept repeating, almost choking on my words.

I was aware of her sitting stiff and silent beside me. Her breathing sounding ragged like it might stop. I wanted to disappear, just vanish in a puff of smoke like in some magic trick.

141

She lifted my chin and looked me in the eyes. I couldn't stand her gaze and tried to turn away, but her grip was firm.

"Tell me everything," she said. Her voice was harsh. There was no warmth, no trace of the gentle mama voice I was used to.

I closed my eyes and fought back tears. I saw Charlie's face, heard his voice, felt his touch and didn't want to tell. I had no choice. Mama was sitting like a statue, waiting.

"It had been a long time since we had seen each other," I finally mumbled, sucking up my tears. "Charlie had changed."

"We all had," Mama said.

"But Charlie seemed . . . different."

"That wasn't an excuse."

"I know, Mama. But he didn't seem like my big brother anymore. He seemed like . . ."

"Like what, Etta?"

"An exciting new person, a stranger, someone I didn't know, someone I wasn't related too, someone I . . . liked."

Mama didn't say anything, just looked at me shaking her head, tears filling her eyes and starting to leak down her cheeks. I couldn't stand being close to her. I got up from the bed and walked across the room to my swing chair, sat down and felt it sway. Mama got up, too, pulled the straight back chair away from my desk and eased into it.

"Help me understand, Etta."

"I can't, Mama. I don't understand myself."

"Try," she demanded.

"It started with just looks," I whispered. "He was always staring at me with this look on his face that made me uncomfortable. Becca told him to stop . . ."

"Rebecca knew about this?"

I shook my head so hard it made me dizzy. "Becca didn't know. She saw him staring at me once and told him to stop. I kept telling him the same thing, but he didn't. He started telling me how much I had changed. I wasn't the same Etta, he said, wasn't even a kid anymore. I was becoming a woman. It was just looks and words, so I tried to ignore his looks and laugh off his words and not pay him any attention."

"When did he do all of this, Etta? I don't recall him saying or doing anything inappropriate."

"He was very careful, Mama, made sure he didn't say or do anything out of place when you or Papa even Becca was around."

"Why didn't you say something?"

"I wanted to but after a while . . . after a while, I started liking what he was saying," I whispered. "It made me feel grown-up, special. Then, things changed."

I stopped and looked at Mama. She seemed to be aging right in front of me, becoming old and haggard. I couldn't read the emotions masking her face and clouding her eyes. How was I going to tell her it made my stomach flip and my breast tingle and created a funny-good feeling all over my body? How was I going to tell her I liked it sometimes? How, how, how was I going to tell her I was pregnant?

"You said things changed, Etta. How?"

"He . . . started . . . touching me.

ETTA

38

It's going to be all right, Etta, Mama said after I finished spilling my guts and I believed her. Unlike Charlie, Mama never lied. It's going to be all right was all she said, her eyes red and swollen, and her face covered in a mask of sadness. Even though I believed her, I couldn't figure out how. She hadn't even told Papa yet. Or was she talking for Papa too?

I kept Mama's words in my mind pulling them out whenever I got scared. But I knew she didn't speak for Papa. It had been days since I blabbed and he hadn't said anything or acted any different. I didn't know what to expect from Papa. He was usually soft-spoken, private with his emotions, only got loud when he was upset. I knew this was going to be one of those times, but I hadn't heard any shouting.

"Have you told Papa?" I kept asking.

Mama never responded, just sighed out loud and looked at me. "I'm still trying to digest all this myself, Etta," she said, after I had asked her for the umpteenth time. "I need to find the right words. To be honest, I don't know how to tell him. Charleston is his pride and joy, and you are his baby. This is going to devastate him."

What about me, I wanted to scream.

She finally told him. She was right. He was devastated.

"Charleston's done something no one else has been able to do," she told me. "He's reduced your father to tears."

I had never seem Papa cry. Never, not even when Mama was so sick we thought she would die. If he cried, it was alone at night behind closed doors. But that's what Mama said. He cried when she told him what Charlie had done.

I couldn't conjure up an image of Papa crying, not my strong Papa. I couldn't stand the thought that Charlie and I had broken his heart, split it in half, right down the middle and left it dripping tears. As hard as I tried, I couldn't get that horrible image out of my head.

Papa wasn't crying when he confronted me. I was in my bedroom, hiding, where I usually was most days. I barely heard the soft tap before the door was easing open and Papa was in my room, closing it behind him. I didn't know what to say.

"Papa."

He leaned against the door, saying nothing, looking at me. He didn't seem angry. He just seemed sad. Very, very sad.

The image of his broken heart popped in my head and I wanted to cry.

He moved quietly away from the door, coming toward me, scaring me, a little.

"Papa," I said, again, trembling.

"I'm going to be very blunt with you, Etta," he said, standing over the bed.

I was wrong, terribly wrong. His voice was quiet but I could almost feel his rage. Papa had never whipped me but I felt that's what he wanted to do now, give me a good whippin. I wanted him to sit down so he would seem less threatening. He didn't. I lowered my head and stared at the floor.

"Look at me," he said. His voice was quiet, but rage seemed to be coming off him in waves.

I did as he said. There was no warmth in his eyes.

"I'm madder than I've ever been in my life, Etta, and my heart hurts and I don't like those feelings. I'm furious at Charleston. The moment your mama's words were out of her mouth, I wanted to kill him. Do you hear me? I wanted to kill my own flesh and blood. God have mercy on my soul, but he had no right, none, to force himself on you, no right to behave like an animal. He wasn't raised to be disrespectful or take advantage of anyone, especially his own sister. I'm also mad at you, Etta. As much as I don't want to, I've got to put a little bit of blame on you. You should have said something. How many times has your mama said you could tell her anything?"

I didn't respond, just concentrated on looking at him.

He sighed and wiped his eyes. "I'm mad at myself, too, I'm even mad at your mama and your sister. We all should have sensed something was wrong." He shook his head and wiped at his eyes again. "I just don't understand it, any of it, how my son could have done such a thing and why you allowed . . . ", he stopped, "why you never said a word."

"I was scared, Papa."

"You were scared." He shook his head again. "You were scared to tell but you weren't scared of what Charleston was doing?"

"Charlie's your favorite," I whispered.

He didn't say anything. Not one word.

And you're right. It wasn't all Charlie's fault, and I liked some of it, I wanted to add.

He eased down beside me. "Maybe I have favored Charleston, but I would never condone this behavior, never. It makes me even sadder that you thought I would."

"Oh, Papa." I was sobbing unable to hold back my tears. I felt his arms around my shoulder, his face and tears against my cheeks. Don't cry, Papa, please don't cry I wanted to tell him. I can't stand to see you cry.

"What's going to happen to Charlie?"

He moved away and stared me in the eyes. "That shouldn't concern you, Etta. Charleston will be taken care of. Trust me."

146

Papa was scaring me again. I felt goose bumps pop out on my skin. I had never seen this side of him. Was this how he was going to react when he found out I was pregnant? I shoved that thought to the back of my mind not wanting to know.

"What do you mean?" I mumbled, still looking at him.

"Your brother is old enough to know all behaviors have consequences, Etta. That's what he's about to find out."

I wanted to ask how, but the look on his face didn't encourage any more questions. I was learning fast about consequences. Because of what I had allowed, Papa was right - I had allowed, Charlie to do, I was going to have a baby at fifteen. What could Papa do to Charlie that could be worse than that?

Mama made an appointment with Dr. Booker.

"Why?" I whined, "I'm not sick."

"I want to make sure you're healthy, Etta. There are certain things you can get from sexual contact."

She must have read the fear in my eyes. "Oh Etta, I thought I had plenty of time to tell you all this before you needed to know," she said squeezing my fingers, "but Charleston's behavior . . ."

"What things, Mama?"

Mama squeezed my fingers tighter. "They're called Venereal Diseases," she said, "and you get them from having sex with someone who has them."

"Charlie . . .?"

"I just want to be sure."

"How do you feel if you have one?"

"I suspect it depends on which one you have, but there would probably be burning or a rash. Maybe some drainage or a bad odor in your private place."

It sounded awful and I was glad it wasn't anything I had, yet.

"Dr. Booker will give you a complete exam, run some tests to make sure you're all right."

"He'll have to look at my private place?"

"Yes, sweetie, inside and out."

Tears gathered in my eyes and dripped down my cheeks.

"And he'll have to make sure you are not pregnant."

"Pregnant?"

Mama nodded. "That can happen too when you have sexual contact."

I stopped listening. I already knew that.

"Have you had your monthly bleeding since . . .?"

I shook my head. "Not yet."

"Oh, Etta," Mama said, again, like they were suddenly the only two words she knew.

Mama and I took the bus to Main Street and walked the two short blocks to Dr. Booker's office. The day was cold and gloomy and it was snowing lightly. The wind blew large fluffy flakes into our eyes and noses and on our lips. I stuck out my tongue and tasted their wetness like I used to do when I was a little girl, wishing I still was. We walked hand in hand not saying a word. I wanted to go back to the bus stop, take the next bus home and forget about seeing Dr. Booker. I didn't need him to tell me I was pregnant. I almost blurted that out to Mama, but I stayed quiet, glad my face was hidden by my stocking cap and scarf.

Dr. Booker's office was in a one-story sturdy brick building nestled amongst plain doll-sized houses. It had long skinny windows and a single glass door with his name painted on it. I hadn't been there since I had gone with Mama for her checkup after she'd gotten over pneumonia. Nothing had changed. The waiting room was still pale green sterile-looking, with ugly uncomfortable armchairs and small wooden tables pushed in between, magazines and papers stacked on top. Several floor lamps were tucked into corners. A carpet with a busy body pattern covered the floor.

The receptionist hadn't changed either. She was old and friendly and had been with Dr. Booker for as long as I could remember. She gave us a wide, open smile, handed Mama some forms and a pen and told us to have a seat. Mama sat right next to the check-in counter and started filling out the papers. I walked across the room and sat in one of the armchairs, trying to act calm, but I was fidgety and my stomach felt queasy. I kept sneaking glances at the receptionist, wondering if she knew. I picked up a frayed *Look* magazine and started flipping through the pages needing something to keep my mind off of why I was there.

I took quick peeks at Mama, too, watched her return the forms and heard the woman tell her doctor would be with us shortly. I watched as she sat back down and unbuttoned her coat, lifting the collar away from her neck. I stared at her. She wasn't Mama anymore. Her smile had disappeared. She looked aged and tired and worn out, like she did after her sickness. Every time I looked at her, I wanted to cry. It was my fault . . . and Charlie's.

The office was filling up with patients, mostly old, mostly women, all white. I felt out of place, like I didn't belong, like I was too young and too colored to be in the same room with them. My mind started having strange thoughts again, wondering if their kind looks and gentle smiles were just cover-ups for what they were thinking. That was ridiculous. How could they know I was pregnant? I was glad I was first on his schedule.

"Etta Netters." The nurse's voice sounded loud and booming, disrupting the quiet, drawing every body's attention, at least that's the way it felt. I got up before she could repeat it, keeping my eyes straight ahead. Mama put her arms around my shoulders as the nurse led us to an exam room.

It was plain and small. A narrow black table covered with harsh white paper, and a flat linen encased pillow placed neatly at the head, sat threateningly in the middle. A metal stand, on wheels, the size of one of Mama's large serving trays, sat at the end, crowded with shiny silver instruments, small clear glass tubes and bottles and rubber gloves. I had never had an exam like this. The nurse handed me a slightly frayed soft cotton gown and told me to undress. I did as I was told, slipped my arms through the sleeves and tied the top back strap. I sat on the edge of the table and tried to cover my bare thighs and legs with the thin flimsy sheet. My body felt stiff as a board and I struggled to stay calm. I wanted to cry like a baby.

The nurse took my blood pressure, my pulse and my temperature. She handed me a paper cup and told me to take it to the bathroom and bring back a urine sample.

"Just stand over the toilet and pee in the cup," she said, seeing my confusion.

To my surprise, I did it.

"Why are you seeing Dr. Booker?" she asked.

"Doctor already knows," Mama interrupted.

She gave Mama a look, said only, "Doctor will be in soon," and left.

"I thought you would be less embarrassed if he knew ahead of time," Mama said, looking at me.

"You told him about Charlie?"

"No, Etta."

"I'm pregnant, Mama."

"I know."

"How . . ."

Mama sucked in her breath, "I'm your mother."

"Now, I don't need to see Dr. Booker, right? We can go home."

She shook her head. "We have to be sure about everything and being pregnant, you'll need to continue to see him."

My heart dropped.

Doctor Booker looked different, very old, very frail and very, very white.

"Anna, nice seeing you again," he said, giving Mama a hug. "You're looking well. How are you feeling?

"I'm fine, Raymond, I'm fine."

I was surprised he hugged Mama, more surprised to hear Mama calling him by his first name. Whenever she talked about him, it was always Dr. Booker, even though he had been our family doctor for a long time.

"Are you sure?" he asked, staring her in the eyes.

Mama nodded and gave him a thin smile.

He looked at her a while longer before turning his attention to me.

"So, young lady, how are you?"

"Fine," I mumbled, unable to look at him, unable to stop my tears and quit acting like a baby.

"Your mother tells me you may be expecting."

I nodded still unable to look at him.

He lifted my chin. "Etta."

I closed my eyes and a sob escaped my throat.

"Look at me, Etta."

Reluctantly I opened them and met his gaze.

"That wasn't so hard was it?"

I cried harder.

"Having a baby is not the end of the world, Etta," he said. "And you are not the first fifteen year old to get pregnant."

By her brother I wanted to ask.

Then, he started talking, explaining what was about to happen and why, the exam, the diseases he would be testing for and the test to tell if I was pregnant. He explained why I needed to be on my back at the edge of the table, my feet in the metal rings sticking out of its sides. He explained why he would be putting instruments and his fingers inside my private part. Vagina he called it.

"This is strange, and embarrassing, and scary," he said, "but it's all necessary."

I was aware of his voice, of Mama standing next to the table practically holding her breath taking in every word, of my body stiffening and starting to tremble.

"Do you understand what I'm saying, Etta?"

I didn't, not all of it, but I nodded anyway.

He walked to the door, called the nurse and sat on the stool at the end of the table. The nurse rolled the tray-on-wheels close to him and placed a funny looking floor lamp over his shoulder bending it low. I couldn't stop trembling.

"Slide all the way down to the edge of the table, Etta," he said, "way down to the edge."

I tried, but it was awkward and the paper was bunching up under me and my legs were beginning to cramp.

"A little more."

I scooted lower. The nurse lifted one leg, putting my foot in the metal rings, then the other, and tried to spread my knees apart.

"Just relax and let them fall open," she said.

Dr. Booker was busy adjusting the light, slipping on gloves and arranging the instruments. "Take a deep breath and try to relax, Etta."

Instead of relaxing I felt my body becoming stiffer, trembling uncontrollably, felt the cramping in my legs getting worse. Mama was squeezing my hand, mumbling something I couldn't understand. I seemed unable to relax. I felt the instrument between my legs. It was cold and hard and hurt just like Charlie. I laid my head on the pillow, bit my lips to keep from crying, but couldn't stop the tears running down the side of my cheeks, soaking the skinny pillow.

"You're doing great, Etta," Dr. Booker said, "I'm almost finished."

Hurry, please hurry was running through my mind.

I felt the instrument sliding out, felt sticky wetness and felt the hurt easing a little.

"I need to check inside one more time."

I felt his hand pressing on my belly and his fingers moving around inside me. It hurt, too, but not as much. Finally, he removed his fingers, pulled off his gloves and tossed them on the tray. "You can get dressed, Etta, I'll be right back."

The nurse freed my feet and helped me straighten out my legs. The cramping was worse. Mama helped me scoot back up to the top of the table, untied my gown and handed me my brassiere, my panties, my wool slacks and sweater. I put them on and slid off the table, stomping my feet hoping to ease the cramps. The nurse quickly cleaned up the mess, gathered all the tubes and bottles and left. She showed no emotions.

"You did good, Etta," Mama said, giving me a hug.

I couldn't look at Mama.

Only one of the tests was positive. I was pregnant, which Mama and I already knew, and Dr. Booker suspected. Now I would have to see him on a regular basis. Mama gathered Papa and Becca around the big wooden table in the kitchen and told them. Becca was hysterical, yelling and screaming, refusing to listen and accusing me of ruining everything. I felt the gap widening between us. Papa was quiet. He showed no reaction at all. I should have been relieved, but Papa had already taught me his quietness was not a true sign of his feelings. I remembered his words about taking care of Charlie and that was before he knew I was pregnant. What would he do now? Papa's quietness was no comfort. Papa still scared me a little.

So, every month, Mama and I took the bus to Main Street and walked the two short blocks to Dr. Booker's office. I expected him to be stern and preachy and judgmental. He wasn't. He was gentle and informative, never once asking me about the father. At my very first visit, he gave me a list of words and their meanings, another list of body parts that would be involved, where they were located and how they worked. He insisted I get familiar, with the lists, so I could learn and understand what was happening to my body. He explained procedures, the importance of eating right and keeping active, talked about my developing baby, fetus he called it, how it looked, what it could do and how much it weighed.

I tried to act like I wasn't interested, but I was fascinated. I was a good student and liked learning new things. I couldn't wait to get into his lists and started looking forward to my visits.

After, Mama took me to lunch, or to the bookstore, or the library, or just window-shopping. She didn't hide me from her friends. It wasn't easy for Mama. I overheard her and Papa talking about the gossip, the questioning about who the father might me, the ugly talk about it's being Papa, which broke my heart, again. They acted like they hadn't heard and tried to ignore it, but I knew it was hurtful.

Becca was a different story. She seldom came home from college. When she did, she ignored me, was more sullen than usual and stayed in her room. Why me, I kept wondering, when Charlie was the one to blame?

CHARLIE

40

Charlie was thinking of dropping out of college and concentrating on his trumpet playing. It wasn't that he didn't like college, he did, and was still a good student, but the trumpet was his first love and he was smart enough to recognize a chance of a lifetime when it was offered. The leader of a popular band had heard him play, taken him on temporarily, trying him out to see if he fit. He fit to perfection and was now playing in classy clubs all over the state instead of the hole-in the wall joints he was used to. The band even traveled out of state and his name was becoming known. People were talking about the young trumpet player, Charlie Netter, the cat that blew his trumpet so sweet he could practically make it sing. He decided to go with Charlie instead of Charleston thinking it sounded less formal and would be easier for people to remember. Yeah, Charlie Netter, trumpeter number one, was on his way. At last his talent was paying off. He was finally getting his big chance. College would have to wait. Besides, he could always go back to college. He hadn't told Papa, yet, and vaguely wondered what he would think. Papa wasn't impressed with him becoming a musician, but Charlie knew it would have no effect on his decision.

Papa.

He had gotten several letters from Papa still singing his praises and missing his assistance and telling him other boring routine family stuff, nothing unusual, which meant his secret was still secret. He hadn't heard from Etta either and had put their summer exploits out of his mind. He wanted to forget them altogether, but they had that funny way of cropping up every now and then.

He was at the bar relaxing, flirting with one of the pretty waitresses, sipping Scotch and feeling good. The evening was young and the band had just finished their first set. The audience was appreciative, crowding the dance floor, cheering and clapping, not wanting them to stop. Charlie took another sip of his drink and glanced around the room. It was a local nightclub, spacious but still intimate, classy, the people dressed to the tee. It was his kind of place. The exact kind of place he had in mind when he dreamed of being a musician. He had grown tired of the raggedy, loud, run-down bars, and was glad those days were behind him. He emptied his glass, slid it across the counter for a refill and pulled out a cigarette. He flicked the head of the match, watched it burst into flames, touched it to the tip, shook it out and dropped it in one of the numerous ashtrays on the counter. He exhaled, fanning smoke away from his face, and noticed an older man across the room walking in his direction. There was something familiar about him. He was dressed in suit and tie and seemed out of place. Charlie was curious.

I know him, popped into his head. He rubbed his eyes like they were playing tricks on him, still fanning away smoke. Papa? No way. Why in the world would Papa be in Tennessee? And why wouldn't he let me know he was coming? He took another look. It **was** Papa. Charlie couldn't believe it. What was he doing here? What was wrong? Etta! His whole body started trembling. Etta had told. She said she wouldn't, had agreed it was their secret, just the two of them and he had believed her. Why had she changed her mind?

"Papa, what are you doing here?" he asked, when Papa reached the bar unable to hide his shock, keeping his voice low and trying to stop trembling.

"We need to talk, Charleston."

He heard the anger in Papa's voice and knew he was in trouble.

"Is Mama sick, again?" he stuttered, trying to sound like he had no idea why Papa had just showed up unannounced.

"I'm playing a gig, Papa. I can't just up and leave."

"Tell whoever you need to tell, Charleston. Be quick about it."

Reluctantly, Charlie whispered something in the pretty waitresses ear and followed Papa out of the club.

"We need to talk," Papa repeated, anger still in his voice.

"Papa, what's wrong? How did you know where to find me?"

"Enough questions. The taxi's waiting."

Charlie held on to his shock and his trembling as the driver drove them to his apartment. All kinds of thoughts were running through his mind. He tried to engage Papa in conversation. But Papa was silent, said not one word, didn't even look at him, just stared straight ahead and acted like he hadn't heard or wasn't listening. So, Charlie shut up.

Once there, Papa changed, became talkative, almost cordial, suggesting he relax and get comfortable. Charlie sighed in relief. This was more like the Papa he was familiar with. Maybe this wasn't going to be as bad as he thought. He slipped out of his jacket and eased into a kitchen chair. Then, Papa changed again, was suddenly behind him, shouting and cussing and shoving his shoulders against the chair, catching him off guard. He was wrapping clothesline around his chest, tying it tight, binding his feet and hands, covering his eyes with a heavy rough cloth. Charlie tired to struggle but it was too late. What the hell was Papa doing? How had he let him con him like this? He knew then he was right. He was in trouble.

"I ought to break your God damn neck," Papa was shouting, "having sex with your own sister and impregnating her."

Charlie felt his heart racing and his stomach turning over, felt bile sting the back of his throat and thought he was going to vomit. Damn, Etta was pregnant. That's why she told. He long ago figured if she told, it would just be her word against his, but she was pregnant. How the hell was he going to deny that?

"Papa, I can . . . "

"Shut up, damn it, I don't want to hear your lies, not a damn one. There's nothing you can say that will excuse your sick behavior."

Papa was leaning over him so close Charlie could feel his spittle on his face. And even though he was in his own apartment not far from friends and colleagues, he felt isolated and disorientated and afraid. Every time he tried to move, the rough line cut into his skin and Papa swatted his legs or arms with a skinny, green switch like he did when he misbehaved as a little boy. He could out fox Papa then. Now he was afraid of him. He had never known Papa to behave this way, yelling and shouting and cussing and breathing heavy. He was glad his eyes were covered so he didn't have to look at his face.

"She was just a baby, Charleston," Papa was still shouting, "just a baby and innocent. Life's cruel realities hadn't yet intruded. She was happy and innocent and carefree, just a kid being a kid. Then you came along and selfishly ruined her life. How could you do that to her? You're a man now, no longer a kid; you need to learn the consequences of your behavior."

Charlie was crying and babbling and his nose was running and snot mingled with tears was dribbling onto his lips.

"I was going to turn your ass into the authorities, but they don't give a shit about a black buck raping his own. So your punishment is left to me, which is fitting, I suppose. Because of me, you've never had to deal with consequences."

159

Suddenly, he felt a cold hardness against his temple. *Papa has a gun?* He started squirming, twisting and turning, shaking his head back and forth struggling to move away almost tipping over the chair. He was still sobbing and babbling confused nonsense. He knew this wasn't happening, Papa holding a gun to his head, he was dreaming, having a nightmare. Papa would never do that, not to his beloved son.

"I'm at fault too," he heard Papa saying, no longer shouting. "I should have held you accountable for your actions. Well, this time I am. It's long over due that you learn consequences can be a real bitch."

Charlie was still twisting and turning and shaking his head. Papa grasped him around the neck, steadied his head against his body, pressed the muzzle firmly against his skull and pulled the trigger.

Charlie heard the click, felt the loosening of his bowels, the warm pee running down his legs, his body convulsing like he was having a fit, surprised he was still breathing. He couldn't believe Papa was playing Russian roulette with his life. Would the next click end it? He was still tense when he felt Papa remove the gun, not sure what he was going to do next. Was he going to kill him or was he playing a cat and mouse game? Charlie was coughing and choking and couldn't breathe. He wanted him to just do it and get it over. He had had enough of his torture.

Papa calmly put the gun back in his pocket, ignored Charlie's babbling and waited for him to stop shaking. He removed the blindfold and loosened his feet and hands. He stared at his son, this son he loved more than life itself, and fought the urge to wipe away his snot and tears, ease his fears and gather him close. He wanted to hug him tight, whisper he loved him, whisper he was forgiven. How in the world was he going to live without his son?

"I'm sorry, Papa, I'm sorry," Charlie was babbling over and over, tears and snot still running down his face and dripping off his chin.

"Look at me," Papa demanded, his voice hoarse.

Charlie raised his head and stared into the eyes of a stranger.

"I am disowning you, Charleston," Papa said. "You are no longer my son and your mother is no longer your mother and your sisters are no longer your sisters. Our home is no longer your home. You are no longer welcomed there. Your name will no longer be mentioned in our house or in our presence. I have cut you out of my will and stopped all my financial assistance. As of this moment, I never want to hear your name or see your face again."

Papa turned on his heels and walked out of the room, quickly, struggling to hold on to his tears. He staggered to the taxi idling at the curb and slipped into the back seat, slamming the door behind him, trying to control his sobs as the driver sped away. He never told anyone, not even his wife, how he had almost killed his son.

Charlie couldn't believe Papa's words, knew he didn't mean them, just knew he would change his mind. He had always been able to play Papa. He sat slumped in the chair ignoring his bruised wrists and ankles, the switch welts all over his arms and legs, his urine and shit-soaked linen pants, the overwhelming, disgusting smell of his body waiting for Papa to walk back through the door. When he didn't, Charlie stayed slumped in his chair.

He must have passed out, wasn't aware of time, had no idea how long he sat stinking and crying. Slowly, he struggled out of the chair, stripped off his soiled clothes and got under a hot shower, scrubbing his skin almost raw. He put on a clean crisp long sleeve white shirt, pressed charcoal linen trousers and slipped his feet into soft leather loafers. He smoothed back his hair, grabbed his trumpet and left. If he hurried, he still had time to rejoin the band and finish the last set.

To hell with Papa, he didn't need his money or him and he certainly didn't need Mama or Rebecca or Etta. He was Charlie Netter, the best trumpet player in the South. He'd show all of them he could make it on his own.

"Hell with you, Papa," he shouted, whistling for a cab and hoping he had enough money for the fare.

ETTA

41

My life was changing, but Mama insisted I keep up my regular routine. I didn't look pregnant and was feeling almost like myself, again. So, I went to school day after day, hung out with Angela and Mavis like everything was normal. If they noticed I was different, and I don't know how they couldn't, they didn't say a thing, not one word. Our talk was about classes, glee club and basketball, but I didn't go to their houses anymore. I blamed it on too much homework and they accepted my lame excuse. They knew something wasn't right but I suspected they were afraid to ask and didn't really want to know.

As I began to get fat, Mama started picking up my assignments and I studied at home in my room or at the dining room table. It was difficult trying to concentrate on schoolwork. I had to read and reread and the information still didn't sink in completely. My mind was too busy with other things. After awhile, Mama stopped getting my lessons. I don't know what she told my teachers. I didn't ask.

My body kept changing too, and I was glad Dr. Booker had given me his lists. My breasts were getting big, hurt when I touched them and my ankles sometimes puffed up at night. My stomach was growing and I could feel the fetus moving around inside. I remember the first time Dr. Booker put my hands on my belly and let me feel the movement. He also let me listen to the heartbeat through his stethoscope. It was such a strange, scary feeling having something alive and breathing and moving around inside me. But I still thought of it as a fetus, never as a baby, my baby.

I was beginning to hate my body and myself. I was miserable and sad and angry and wanted to kill Charlie. That thought scared me.

I had never wanted to hurt anyone, no less kill them. But if Charlie walked through my bedroom door, I would want to kill him.

That was never going to happen again. Papa had taken a trip South and read him the riot act. I wondered if Papa wanted to give him a good whippin too, even wondered if he had? If he did, he didn't tell us, just told us he had banned Charlie from our lives. Mama, Becca, and I couldn't believe Papa actually disowned his son, whom he loved more than life itself. He was in misery, grieved over him like he was dead. His face was haggard and he seemed old and listless. I couldn't stand it. I wanted to yell and scream, go crazy. How could Charlie and I have been so careless, so selfish and cause all this chaos and heartache?

"I hope you're satisfied," Becca screamed stomping into my room after Papa told us. "You're as much to blame as Charleston."

"I had no say in Papa's decision, Becca. He didn't ask for my advice."

"No, all you did was cry and blamed everything on Charleston."

"No I didn't. I admitted I was at fault too."

"When it was too late. Why didn't you say something before it got out of hand, Etta?"

"I was scared, Becca."

"Sacred of what?"

"Papa, you know Charlie . . ."

"You know what I think?"

I don't care what you think I wanted to yell. I just wanted her out of my room. She wasn't Papa or Mama. I didn't have to explain anything to her.

"I think you liked it, that's what. You liked Charleston's attention and liked him fondling all over you."

"Think what you want," I finally shouted, tired of listening.

"Then when it got out of hand," she said, ignoring what I said, "and you could no longer control him, you yelled rape."

"I never used that word, Becca, even though that's what it was."

"It's not rape if you went along with it, Etta. You're smart enough to know that."

"Why are you mad at me and not Charlie?"

"Cause you could have prevented it, all of it, the whole ugly mess, if you had only told," she yelled, running out of my room and slamming the door.

Her words felt like a slap in the face. I wanted to run after her, tell her I was sorry I had messed up our lives. Instead, I flopped down on my bed and cried until I had no more tears.

Unlike Becca, Mavis and Angela were trying to stay in touch, which surprised me. I figured their parents would forbid them to have anything to do with me. I should have known better. Their parents were still friends with Papa and Mama, not part of the gossiping crowd. Mavis and Angela were hanging in there or trying to. They called on the phone but I wouldn't talk. They sent me notes that I didn't answer. They showed up at the door but I didn't want to see them. I begged Mama to tell them I was sleep or busy or any excuse. Of course she didn't. Mama was not into lying. She showed them to my room and closed the door. They stood just inside staring at me. Then, they were all over me hugging and crying and trying to talk at the same time.

"We've missed you," Mavis said, wiping her eyes.

"More than you'll ever know, Etta," Angela said, wiping at hers too.

I couldn't talk, I was crying too hard.

"Why didn't you want to see us?" Mavis whined, sitting beside me and playing with her hair.

"I'm fifteen and pregnant," I mumbled, trying to stop crying.

"But, we're your friends. Besides, it wasn't your fault."

I sucked up my tears and wiped at my eyes.

"Etta," Mavis said, looking at me.

I kept wiping my eyes, ignoring her words.

She was still looking at me, waiting for me to respond.

"I didn't know you had a boyfriend," Angela said, fidgeting in her chair and stealing a glance at Mavis. "Do we know him?"

I shook my head.

"It was mostly his fault right, like Mavis said?" Angela was staring at me too.

"It was both our faults," I finally said.

"How does it feel being pregnant?" she asked, hesitantly touching my belly.

"Awful." I envied their skinny bodies and wanted mine back.

"Is it scary?" she asked.

"Yes."

"How did it feel?" Mavis asked.

"I just told you."

"I mean, how did, you know, feel?"

"What?"

"The," her face was turning red, "sex."

"Mavis," Angela said, shock in her voice, "that's none of your business."

"Angela's right," I mumbled. How could I tell her it made my stomach feel funny good, caused tingling in my breast and between my legs? "It's none of your business."

"Did you like it?" she persisted.

166

When did Mavis get so bold?   But since she had gotten up enough nerve to ask, I figured I had enough to be honest. Besides, I was tired of lying. "Sometimes," I whispered.

The silence was awkward. Mavis's was staring at me in wide-eyed shock, her face still red. Angela was fidgeting in her chair, again, and looking at the floor. And I just wanted them to go. We no longer had anything in common.

ETTA

42

Nine months seemed like forever. I was scared of having a baby, but I wanted it over. I knew it was going to hurt, bad, and I was going to cry, be more of a baby than the fetus inside me. I wanted to ask Mama but I wasn't sure I really wanted to know and not sure I wanted to put any more misery on her. I had already given her more than her share. She and Papa were still upset and worried and Becca was still mad. I wanted it over.

I was tired of being big and awkward, feeling ugly and crying my eyes out. I was tired of the backs of my legs bunching up in knots and my feet puffing over my shoes. I was tired of my belly stretched out of shape and not being able to touch my toes. I was tired of huffing and puffing walking the short distance to the bus stop, of seeing Dr. Booker every month, soon every week, and going through the day to day realities of his lists. I was tired of living with the daily reminder of what Charlie had done, especially now that the fetus was alive and active. I was tired of being pregnant.

I was tired of seeing that haggard look on Mama's face, too, and the sadness in her eyes, tired of seeing Papa walking around like he was lost because he had cut off all connection with his son. I was tired of Becca being constantly mad because Charlie was no longer a part of our family. I was tired of wondering how I could fix it, put it all back like it was, knowing I couldn't. I was tired of being tired.

I just wanted it over!

But, I was scared, too, scared of having a baby and being a mama. I didn't know how to do either and didn't want to learn. I didn't want all that grown-up responsibility. I wanted to have fun, go to school, to the movies with Angela and Mavis and sit in the swing on the wrap-around porch writing poetry. I wanted to read books and practice the piano. I wanted to be a kid of fifteen, again.

I wanted, needed, to quit whining. I was tired of that too.

Becca was home for the weekend. I wanted to knock on her bedroom door and try to make it right between us. I missed her. Mama kept telling me to give it time. She would come around eventually. As much as I wanted to believe Mama, I couldn't. Becca was never the forgiving type. I was curious about Becca. How was she doing in college? Did she like it? What classes was she taking? What did she want to be and how hard was it, really? Had she made friends, was she having fun? Will I ever get to college?

As much as I didn't want to, I wondered about Charlie, too. Was he still living in the South, how was he getting by without Papa's money, was he still playing his trumpet. Did he ever think about that day in the park, about me? Will I ever see him again?

How is all of this going to end?

I had to give it to Mama and Papa. They were mad at me, too, but unlike Becca, didn't keep throwing it up in my face. Mama was busy sewing cute doll-size sleepers and undershirts and blankets in all different colors and taking me shopping at Sears for all the baby stuff she couldn't make. Papa got a beautiful old crib, rocking chair, and chest of drawers from one of his clients, spent hours stripping off the paint, staining and polishing them to their original beauty. Mama lined the drawers with colorful paper and made curtains to match. My room was getting crowded. I was beginning to feel closed in or maybe pushed out. I wanted to whine about that, too, but Mama and Papa were way past their breaking point.

ETTA

43

The cramping woke me. I was dreaming of summer and swimming and eating wieners roasted over an open fire. Papa was there and Mama and Becca and Charlie. We were at the lake not far from our little town. Papa had rented a house right on the water. We had gotten up early and packed the car. Charlie drove. Papa sat up front and me and Becca, with Mama in between, sat in the back. The sun was hot, not a cloud in the sky, a gentle breeze teased our skin, making it almost bearable. We sat in lawn chairs on the deck and dabbled our bare feet in the warm clear water, talking and laughing and eating roasted wieners and marshmallows on a stick.

Then the cramping started nudging me awake. I tried to ignore it and hold on to the dream, but it was persistent. At first, it felt like my monthly bleeding like Dr. Booker said it would, familiar but different. I lay still breathing deeply trying to relax and absorb the pain, easing it a little. I closed my eyes and slipped back into my dream, the hot sun on the clear sparkling water, the smell of roasted wieners and marshmallows, the sounds of happy talk and laughter. The cramping intruded again making me squirm. I tried not to cry.

I awkwardly struggled out of bed, turned on the bedside lamp and hobbled to my swing chair. It was too early, but Dr. Booker said first babies sometimes came early. I leaned back in the chair causing it to sway, pressed my head against its side and closed my eyes. The cramping stopped. I tiptoed back to bed.

I woke up, wanting to scream. The cramping was back. I felt like throwing up. I struggled out of bed again, tried to hurry to the bathroom, stood gagging over the toilet for how long I don't remember, flushed the stool and hobbled back to bed. This was it. I was about to get my wish.

The pattern continued, cramping, easing, dozing, cramping. I was up at daylight worn out by the routine. The fetus seemed to be copying my behavior, moving restlessly inside me. I vaguely wondered if it was a girl or boy. Mama insisted it was a girl because of the way I was carrying it she said. Dr. Booker put no stock in that, thought it was more likely a boy. Papa and Becca gave it no thought at all. They were not into guessing. Nothing about this was a game, as if I didn't know.

Mama confirmed I was in labor, assured me it was going to take a while, all day probably even into the next. She gently reminded me it was going to get worse before getting better and assured me I had plenty of time before needing to go to the hospital.
She called Dr. Booker anyway, putting him on notice.

As hard as I tried, I couldn't get comfortable. Mama made me clear soup and Jell-O and hot tea. I was hungry but afraid to eat. I tried to read but couldn't hold onto the words. I even tried playing the piano hoping to relieve some of my panic. Nothing helped. Mama encouraged me to keep active, walked me up and down the stairs, back and forth down the hall, and around and around the wrap-around porch. Papa came home early, asking if there was something he could do.

Make it go away, Papa, please make it go away.

By the next day, I was so scared my body was shaking, going from cold to hot and the contractions were beginning to feel more like pain. I still felt sick to my stomach too, and my bowels were loose. Mama decided it was time. Papa drove us to the hospital.

The room was small and cold and without windows. Strange looking stuff lined the walls but the bed was just a bed like my bed at home not scary at all. I still couldn't stop shaking. The nurse was nice, treated me like the kid I was, and tried to ease my fears. My water broke and I thought I had peed the bed even though I knew this was going to happen. I had forgotten.

They moved me to the delivery room with the too bright lights, strange looking machines and sounds and smells. I was scooted onto a skinny table with metal hoops at the end like the one in Dr. Booker's office. Dr. Booker was there, calm and soothingly gentle, still guiding me through it, naming body parts and instruments and explaining everything he was doing. He kept pressing on my belly, seeing if my baby was moving down into my pelvis, putting his fingers in my vagina, checking how much my cervix had opened or dilated. I wanted to hold onto Mama, but she and Papa were restricted to the waiting room, not allowed in this sterile space. It hurt, hurt, hurt like I knew it would and I tried not to cry. Nurses dressed in long white gowns and caps and gloved hands and masks that covered their mouths and noses moved in and out of the room, timing my contractions and listening to the baby's heart thru the stethoscope they placed on my belly. They gave me something for pain that made me feel kind of funny and confused and didn't help much. It was scary, seemed like something out of a horror movie. Everyone was in constant motion. So much was going on I couldn't keep up.

I wanted to push.

"Not yet, Etta," the nurse said, her words sounding muffled, "doctor's giving your baby more room to come out."

I forgot about the cutting. The pain was bad, really, really bad, and steady. I kept thinking if only I could push it would feel better but she kept saying not yet. I was crying, even though I didn't want to, acting like a baby again, and talking nonsense. Where is Mama? I want Mama.

"It's almost over, Etta."

172

I heard Dr. Booker's voice and tried to start acting like a grown-up, not wanting to embarrass him. But it hurt . . . bad!

"Push," the nurse finally said.

She kept saying it over and over even Dr. Booker was saying it. Relieved I had permission, I started pushing and pushing and pushing. I felt my baby moving down the birth canal; felt it between my legs, wiggling on my belly. I heard its cry. I started to relax. The worst was over.

"It's a boy," Dr. Booker said.

A boy, what was I going to do with a baby boy? Panic started creeping into my body again. It wasn't over. It was just beginning.

Mama and Papa were waiting when I got to my room. Mama was crying and Papa was trying not to.

"He's beautiful, Etta," Mama said giving me a kiss on the cheek.

"And healthy," Papa said. "He has all his fingers and toes and a head full of hair.

I tried to tune them out. I didn't want to hear about the baby.

"Have you seen him?" Mama was asking.

I lied and shook my head. I had seen him but only a quick look.

"That's an easy fix," Papa said, pressing the call button before I could stop him.

"I'll bring him right in," a woman's voice responded.

Take your time, I wanted to tell her, there's no rush.

She didn't. She was soon coming through the door, smiling and placing a small swaddled bundle in my arms.

"If you need me, just press the button again."

Don't leave I wanted to yell, but the door was already closing behind her. I pulled the blanket away from my baby's face, my baby, and stared at him, relieved he didn't look anything like Charlie or me. He was kind of a faded-brown and wrinkled and tiny, so tiny and his head was big, so big and looked out of shape and his eyes were squeezed shut. Mama lied. He wasn't beautiful. He was ugly.

"Didn't I tell you he was beautiful?" she said again.

I didn't respond. No way could I call Mama a liar.

"You need to give him a name, Etta," Papa said.

A name, what I was going to name him had never crossed my mind. I was too busy trying to deny he was even inside me. But he was, of course, and now that he was here, I couldn't deny him any longer, and he did need a name. How about Charleston Epstein Netter, Jr.? That's who he really was, but that would be hurtful and Mama and Papa would not be amused. A name, a name, what would be a nice proper name for a baby who was fathered by his uncle, a product of rape and born out of wedlock? He needed a strong, elegant important sounding name to get around all of that. Malcolm popped into my head.

"Malcolm," I said, staring at him. "Your name is Malcolm."

"Malcolm," Mama said, rolling it around on her tongue. "I like it. What do you think, Jonas?"

"Malcolm, hmm, that'll do," Papa said.

ETTA

44

Being pregnant was bad, but the healing afterwards was bad too. Postpartum was what Dr. Booker called it.

"You're now in your postpartum period, Etta."

Gentle old Dr. Booker was still adding words to the vocabulary list he'd insisted I learn, a vocabulary I knew I would never share with Angela and Mavis because it consisted of words like vagina, uterus, labor, contractions, cervix, dilate, stethoscope, placenta, delivery, episiotomy. And I had learned them all, what they were, where they were and how to say them right. I was surprised knowing them actually worked, helped me understand what was happening to my body, making my pregnancy a little less scary. I guess there really was a reason for his insistence.

Now here was postpartum and like all the words before it, postpartum hurt. My body had no shape; my stomach was flat again but flabby like some old woman's and hurt and the nurses kept massaging and pressing on it to get the uterus back where it belonged they said. The bleeding and cramping were worse than my monthly bleeding and I had to sit in a tub of warm water, two, three times a day to help heal the stitches. They kept waking me up in the middle of the night to take my temperature, press on my belly or check my bleeding.

And then there was breastfeeding. They woke me up in the middle of the night for that too. Everyone, Dr. Booker, the nurses, even Mama wanted me to at least try. It's the best thing for your baby they all insisted. So I did and it was a disaster. It hurt and my breasts were sore and swollen and I didn't like Malcolm that close. I couldn't get the hang of it either. Neither could he. I cried from frustration. He cried from hunger. It slowly dawned on them it wasn't working. They

175

started him on formula. He took to the bottle greedily. They bound my breast to help dry up the milk, but they still leaked and my chest stayed sticky with their pale, watery liquid.

I was glad when Dr. Booker finally let me go home. Mama still bound my breast and I still sat in the tub two, three times a day, but it was good being home, in my own room and my own bed. The only problemwas Malcolm. He was in my room too and I was afraid of Malcolm. He was little, his movements were jerky and he had no control of his head that seemed way too big for his tiny body. When I picked him up it flopped backwards and he almost wriggled out of my arms. He made strange noises, strange faces, sometimes choked when I fed him, spit up milk, and constantly pooped and peed. His breathing was funny too, kind of fast and seemed off beat. I was afraid I'd find him dead or dying in his crib. And he cried, a lot, and I didn't know why, was he hungry, did he hurt, want to be held, cuddled, loved, what?

Dr. Booker and Mama tried to assure me all of this was natural, my baby was healthy, tougher than he seemed, and I would get used to his cues, Dr. Booker'sword. As hard as I tried, I didn't believe them. Mama was my rescuer. She soothed his crying, cuddled and loved him when she gave him his bottle, hummed softly while she waited patiently for him to burp. That was the way I wanted to be with him, but I couldn't. He scared me and every time I looked at him, I saw Charlie.

Mama seemed to understand. She never pressured me or got on my case for not taking more care of him. But she worried I wasn't bonding, another one of doctor's words, with him. She mentioned it to Papa, even Dr. Booker.

"Give her time," they said, "time to get used to him."

Becca was another story. The few times she came home, she fumed and fussed at me and . . . Mama.

"Why are you always the one feeding Malcolm?" she yelled, her voice full of anger, "he's Etta's baby. Why isn't she feeding him, washing and changing his diapers, making his formula and getting up in the middle of the night?"

"Watch your tone and your tongue, Rebecca," Papa scolded.

"You know I'm right, Papa," she said, staring at him with tears in her eyes.

"Oh, Rebecca," Mama said, giving her a smile, trying to ease her anger, "I'm giving Etta a little time to adjust and get comfortable with being a mother."

My heart hurt for Becca. I wanted to cry too, hug her tight and tell her she was right, I was the one who should be doing the work and caring for Malcolm. But I didn't want to be a mother. I didn't know how and didn't want to learn, no less get comfortable with it. I just wanted to be a kid, again. I didn't want the grown-up responsibility of caring for a baby. I was glad and relieved and, I admit, guilty Mama was willing to do it. But Becca was right. He was my son . . . and Charlie's. Everyone seemed to forget that. He was Charlie's son too. Why did I have to be a mama when he didn't have to be a papa?

Charlie. Had anybody bothered to contact Charlie? I desperately wanted to know, but was afraid to ask since the mention of his name was forbidden. I couldn't stop my thoughts though. What would he think about me having his son from what he had done was always in the back of my mind? But I knew he wouldn't care, would even try to deny it. He certainly wouldn't want people to know he had sex with his sister. It was not only a sin; it was a crime. I was finally grasping the truth about Charlie. How could I have been so stupid?

Dr. Booker, Mama, and Papa were right. With time I got over my fears and started understanding when Malcolm was hungry or wet or sleepy or just needed some quiet time. I stopped seeing Charlie every time I looked at him, too, just saw a darling; loveable baby that was my son and started bonding with him, tried loving him like his

177

mother. I changed, fed and cuddled him more often, even hummed while waiting for him to burp, like Mama. Sometimes, I just held him close and whispered sweet nothings in his ears and marveled at his presence. It felt strange, at first, and scary, but I slowly got used to him even started enjoying him, a little. To my surprise, so did Becca. She never said a word, just one day when he was about six months she heard him crying, picked him up, changed his diaper, sat in the rocking chair holding him close and fed him his bottle. From then on, she was hooked, started easily reading his cues, even babysat on occasion and began coming home on weekends and holidays again. It puzzled me how she could despise me and love my son. But she did, she truly loved Malcolm, treated him like a little brother and later, like one of her own. I wanted her to treat me like her baby sister again, too, but she didn't.

I missed Becca, missed her sullen ways and know-it-all attitudes, her whining and complaining. I tried hard to get us back on that old familiar path, but she would have none of it. She stayed distant and mad, continued to treat me like the enemy. I decided I would have to live with her punishment.

Mavis and Angela were so excited about my baby they practically moved into our house. They were fascinated with Malcolm, curious about all his baby ways and played with him for hours, like some favorite toy. They seemed more comfortable with him than I was. I kept thinking it was because he wasn't theirs. They weren't stuck with him all day every day, day after day after day, and could leave when they got bored or tired.

But, I was happy to see them, glad we were reconnecting, making my life seem a little more like normal. I had missed them and it was fun to talk about school and music and basketball, again, instead of baby this and baby that. It was spring and school would soon be out and the hot lazy days of summer were right around the corner and maybe we could go to the movies or the park or just sit in the swing on the wrap-around porch like we used to, pretending we were still on the same track. Although I had changed, they hadn't. Angela was still quiet, and Mavis was still Mavis, asking all her twenty thousand questions.

"How did it feel having a baby, Etta?"

What a stupid question. How do you think it felt? It hurt, a lot. That's what I wanted to tell her. I didn't. I didn't want to hurt her feelings. She was just being curious and meant no harm. Besides, if things were reversed I would probably wonder about that too. I had to admit it was a fair question but not one I wanted to keep answering.

"It's not something I would recommend at fifteen," I said.

She laughed, turned red, and quit asking.

I liked having them around. It was almost like the days before Malcolm. We giggled and gossiped and argued over nonsense. They were studying for exams and practicing hard with basketball. Their team was going to the championship tournaments in the city. I couldn't hide my envy, hated Charlie again for the umpteen time. Thanks to Mama and Papa, I did get to one game. Mama babysat and Papa took me. It was fun and exciting and I yelled and screamed until I was hoarse and wished I was still a part of it.

Their team came in second.

Malcolm was a happy, content baby, good-natured. I always wondered where he got that from, probably not from Charlie or me. He was healthy, too, seldom got colds or fevers or diarrhea or any of the awful things babies got.

Dr. Booker was fascinated with him. He treated him special and bragged about how bright he was to his staff. Mama laughed, said it

179

was because he didn't follow many colored babies, probably thought they were different somehow, but wasn't sure, didn't quite know what to expect. I tended to agree with Mama. I think Dr. Booker knew he was Charlie's though. I don't know if Mama finally told him or he just figured it out, but I think he knew.

As Malcolm got older, I wondered if anyone else had.

Unfortunately, my love of learning and books and reading didn't rub off on Malcolm. He was just a fair student, preferred working with his hands instead of getting lost between the pages of a book. He loved taking things apart and putting them back together. He could fix anything and seemed to have a natural talent for it. It fascinated Papa. Papa wasn't hands on. When things broke, he had to call someone to fix them. He admired that in Malcolm, liked the fact he could figure out what was wrong and fix it. Malcolm loved sports, too, especially football. He was solid and husky, physically suited for the game. Mama and I were always afraid he would get hurt, but he never did, at least not anything serious, Papa and Malcolm, two opposites that really attracted. What would Charlie have thought of that?

CHARLIE

45

Quitting college had been the right decision for Charlie. The band had taken off, playing not only in the South, but also all over the east coast. And Charlie was becoming its star. He was earning a good salary and money was becoming less and less of a problem. He was slowly recovering from the lack of Papa's financial assistance.

Charlie was a musical genius, truly born to play the trumpet. He not only loved it, he lived it, all day every day. He practiced for hours experimenting with all kinds of music, jazz, blues, even messing around with the classics creating his own style and had been approached about recording an album, which excited him. He was thinking of moving back to the Midwest. He had gotten an offer he couldn't refuse in the Windy City, playing with an even bigger band. He wouldn't be the star, at least for a while, but he figured he could live with that. So much was happening in his life, he couldn't help but wonder what Papa would think of him now.

Papa. Occasionally, he thought about Papa and Mama and Rebecca and even Etta. He would instinctively pick up the phone when something new and exciting happened before remembering. He had to admit he missed them and was curious about how they were doing. Did they ever think about him, were curious about him and missed him too? He tried not to think too much about Etta. Papa had accused him of ruining Etta's life. He didn't want to admit Papa was probably right. How had he been so careless? He should have left Etta alone but she was so tempting, so ripe for the picking. He had conveniently put Etta out of his mind, shoved her into the past, a past that no longer had anything to do with him. And since Papa had disowned him, never wanted to see or hear from him again, it was easy to dismiss what he had done, even deny it had ever happened and move on with his life.

His life was changing. He met a woman, a classy educated older woman who was attractive, smart and sophisticated. She was the kind of woman he was looking for. The only hitch, she had a son by a previous lover. Charlie wasn't into kids. He was too selfish and egotistical, always put himself first. Fortunately, the boy lived with his father, only had random visits with his mother, making her and Charlie's relationship workable.

Her name was Millie. She was tall and elegant, lightskinned, like him, aloof and snobbish. She was the perfect mate. She loved he was a musician, loved music and traveling with the band. The other members grumbled about her presence since their wives or lovers weren't allowed on the bus or train. But Charlie Netter was the man, the main attraction. He was afforded special privileges kind of like in the good old days with Papa.

Charlie took the gig in Chicago, married Millie and became famous. His albums were in the record stores and played on the radio and the band even got minor parts in several films playing at some make believe white high society affair. Charlie was attractive, looked good on screen, and loved all of it. This was how life was supposed to be. He knew Papa had to know about his success, but still he wanted to call him, just for the hell of it, and couldn't count the number of times he almost did. He knew what he would say, too, always carried the words in his head.

"Papa, this is Charleston, remember me, the son you disowned? What do you think of me now that I'm rich and famous?"

182

He wanted to shove it down Papa's throat and gag him with his success. As hard as he tried, he couldn't forget Mama and Rebecca and Etta and would never forgive Papa for casting them out of his life. Funny thing though, he still loved Papa.

ETTA

46

When Mama and Papa started talking about my returning to school, I didn't want to hear it. Even though I was a good student, I had been gone too long, was way behind, and wasn't sure I could catch up. I was afraid of what my teachers would think, too, what they had heard and how they would react. I wanted to go. I loved school and learning and missed it. I always got envious when I overheard Becca telling Mama and Papa about college, how much she liked it, how fun it was and how she wanted to stay for graduate school. Her words surprised me. Becca wasn't outgoing, didn't make friends easily, but I was glad she was having fun and there was some happiness in her life. I wanted to be like Mavis and ask twenty thousand questions because that's what I wanted to do, too, but Becca wasn't talking to me so I kept all my questions bottled up in my head. The one thing I knew for sure, I had to finish high school and Mama and Papa were sounding like they were willing to give me that chance.

When I told Angela and Mavis, they were excited and laughed when I said I was scared.

"Don't be silly, Etta, you're smart, you can do it. Besides we'll help," they said, giving me a hug. They were now ahead of me but still had a year left. I knew then Angela and Mavis and I would be friends forever even though they would be off to college and I'd be stuck in high school.

I fumbled with the long gray robe and placed the stiff funny shaped hat on my head. A grin kept forming on my lips and I fought back tears that were wetting my cheeks as I squeezed into line and began the slow march down the aisle. I couldn't believe I was actually graduating from high school. I dabbed at my eyes, took a deep breath and searched the crowd until I saw them. Mama was dabbing at her eyes too, Papa was all grins and Becca was fiddling withMalcom, a frown on her pretty face. I struggled again with my tears and held my head high knowing the sacrifices they had made to get me this far. I even heard Mama's voice in my ear.

"You've made us proud, Etta."

Her words made me feel guilty. I didn't deserve them. That's what I should have been saying to her and Papa, even Becca. They were the ones who had made this possible and deserved all the credit. They were the ones who saved me.

Becca made it too. She had her graduate degree and a good job, so Mama and Papa said it was my turn and offered to pay for my continuing schooling. I wanted to say yes. That had always been my dream. I said no. It didn't feel right me continuing to be dependent on them. Besides, I had more than used up my education money. I went to clerical school instead, got a job, not as good as Becca's, but a job, and started paying my own way.

I confess I wasn't the best mother to Malcolm. Even though I loved him, I couldn't get that close. I could never quite separate him from Charlie. I tried, Mama knew I tried, but it never seemed like he belonged to me. From the day he was born, Mama and Papa became his parents. They ignored the gossip and raised him like their own, took on total responsibility. They clothed him, fed him and paid for his doctor visits. They raised him in the church, too, just like us. Every Sunday they took him to Sunday school and stayed for eleven o'clock service. When he got older, Papa took him to choir practice and young peoples' gatherings. Both Mama and Papa went to school meetings, talked with his teachers and Papa even came home early sometimes to take him to his after school activities. Malcolm became attached to them, especially Papa, followed him around like he was his shadow and cried when he got left behind. Papa spoiled him rotten, too, just like he did Charlie . . . and me and Becca. IPapa was missing Charlie, saw him in Malcolm, was remembering Charlie as a little boy. Malcolm helped fill that gap. That's probably why he and Papa were inseparable.

Everyone conveniently ignored the truth that Malcolm was my son. I was grateful but sometimes, as we all got older, my guilt got in the way. I felt bad I had put all that misery on them and Charlie had gotten off scot-free. I suspected Mama and Papa took on the job of raising Malcolm because they knew I couldn't. I also suspected they felt responsible for Charlie's behavior, felt guilty that he not only robbed me of my childhood, but also ruined my life.

Papa died from a stroke when Malcolm was a teenager. He woke early one morning drooling, babbling, confused, his right arm and leg flopping uselessly. We did a deathwatch for three long awful days before he finally gave up the ghost. Poor Malcolm was totally lost, cried like his heart was broken and would never mend. I grieved for Papa. I could never repay my debt to Papa. I grieved for Malcolm too. I could never re-write his birth history either.

Charlie actually showed up for Papa's funeral with his wife and stepson. How ironic, I thought, a stepson when he had a son of his own. Although it was never mentioned, he knew I had gotten pregnant. I still remembered that day in my bedroom when Papa said he was going to teach him the consequences of his behavior. I never doubted Papa's words. Papa didn't say things he didn't mean.

Now here he was acting like nothing had happened. I couldn't believe his gall. How did he even know Papa was dead? Mama admitted she called and told him. She also admitted Papa kept up with Charlie. He knew all about his success, knew he was living in the capital city just down the highway, had been for sometime, but never made any effort to call or see him. I kind of suspected that. I couldn't see Papa completely losing track of his son.

"Your Papa was serious about disowning him, Etta, but he was still his son, my son. I prayed long and hard and cried a whole lot of tears before making my decision," she said, "I didn't encourage him one way or the other, I just felt in my heart he should know."

"You know Mama's right, Etta. Papa was his papa too," Becca said.

I wasn't surprised Becca agreed. She was still blaming me, but I wanted no part of Charlie. Even after all these years, I wanted no part of Charlie. What I wanted was to scream and holler and have a fit. Why couldn't Mama leave well enough alone?

"He's meeting me . . . us at the church," she said, slight defiance in her voice.

I looked at Mama. I could almost see all those tears spilling out of her eyes, running down her cheeks and dripping off her chin. As much as I wanted to disagree, argue, defend my side of her decision, I couldn't. I swallowed my words. There was no way I could disrespect Mama.

He hadn't changed. He was still attractive and charming and arrogant, tried to act like his coming home after fifteen long years was natural. My feelings were all mumbo-jumbo. He wasn't the Charlie of my fifteenth year, of course, but he still seemed like that brother, the brother that took advantage of my innocence. I was uncomfortable and awkward and felt dirty and guilty all over again. I wanted to run away from his presence. I couldn't. We were burying Papa. So, I kept sneaking peeks at him and Malcolm trying to see if there was any resemblance. Of course there was, but just a little, the mouth and around the eyes. I prayed no one else noticed.

187

Although I didn't argue, I had to admit, I was mad at Mama, wished she hadn't called. Charlie didn't deserve to be here, sitting right next to her, sobbing over Papa like he had been the perfect son. I could feel my anger churning like acid in the pit of my stomach, making me sick. I also prayed it didn't spew out.

Mama cried like her heart was broken and would never mend, too. I think as much over seeing Charlie as Papa dying. Was losing a son as hard as losing a husband? I truly grieved for Mama, but I couldn't feel sorry for Charlie. Charlie had brought all this suffering not only on himself but also on us. I was relieved when the service was over, relieved he didn't linger, didn't even go to the gravesite, just gave Mama a hug, gathered his wife and stepson and left. I couldn't help wondering if Charlie was ever going to get his true punishment?

Mama wasn't Mama for a long while after Papa died. She was listless, walked around in a trance and her smile disappeared again. Sweet, sweet Mama couldn't adjust to living without her Papa of so many years. I became Mama's caregiver. It felt good to be giving instead of receiving. Friends were there for Mama, but Mama was too proud to show them her true grief. She put on her stoic face whenever they came calling and I protected her privacy like she had protected mine. Becca was working in another state but came home as often as she could and put aside her anger, temporarily. Charlie called, occasionally, talked only to Mama, but Mama never encouraged him to visit, for which I was grateful. Slowly, Mama got back to almost being Mama. She said Papa's dying had left a permanent unfixable hole in her heart that nothing could fill.

ETTA

47

I stop my words. My face is wet with tears and I know my story is finished, at least the story I kept hidden in my mind all these years. The story I was too ashamed to tell, that ruined my life and validated my ignorance, my naiveté the summer I turned fifteen. The story that confirmed Charlie's fatherhood and his crime and documented Malcolm's true identity. The story Francesca unknowingly encouraged me to share.

Mama, Papa, Charlie and Becca, I can't help but wonder how different our lives would have been if the summer of my fifteenth year had been like all the others. Would Charlie have been an active part of the family or would he have done some other horrifying thing that would ban him from our lives? As I said, Charlie was Charlie. Would Becca and I have become closer? Maybe but I doubt it. Would Papa have lived longer? Probably not, when God's ready for you circumstances don't matter. Would I have followed in Becca and Charlie's footsteps and gone to college? You bet I would. Would I have married and had kids? Maybe, but not a son called Malcolm, I know that for sure. Malcolm was a chosen name, created from difficult circumstances, belonging to one very special person. Would I have been happy? Only God knows, it's so hard to define happiness, but I can always hope. It's all water under the bridge now, but still I wonder.

The whining tape finally registers in my mind and I turn off the machine, glad it will no longer be a part of my life. I wipe at my tears with the back of my hand, sit quiet, motionless while all kinds of memories continue to run through my mind. I close my eyes and see

Malcolm, big and strong and gentle, with teasing ways and a heart full of love, so different from Charlie. He was a family man, loved kids but had none of his own just married a woman with a house full, my sweet, sweet Malcolm.

I close my eyes and see me and Papa and Mama and Becca even Charlie dressed up formal eating dinner at the dining room table.

I close my eyes and see Charlie.

I feel my tears again.

I can almost smile now when I think of my pregnancy and gentle old Dr. Booker who died not long after Malcolm's second year. I still have his lists hidden in the back of Malcolm's baby book. They are yellow and faded and almost unreadable but that doesn't matter. I don't need to read them anymore. The words are not new and scary and I'm long past fifteen. Besides, I memorized them, long ago, and they are still imprinted on my brain. I used to pull them out, though, pull them out and just stare at the words. I finally stopped. I didn't need those memories roaring back like it was only yesterday, me at fifteen, in the park no bigger then a field, lying on a blanket with Charlie.

Like Dr. Booker told me, I wasn't the first fifteen year old to get pregnant, but that's what it felt like at the time, at least to me. Now days, girls even younger than fifteen are getting pregnant and having babies like it's nothing special, strut around like it's something to be proud of, no shame at all or opt for abortions. Maybe that's a good thing, better than letting it ruin their lives like me. Or, maybe they just haven't gotten to that stage yet. Who am I to judge? I do wonder how many are the results of incest, though, brothers like Charlie forcing themselves on their young innocent sisters? I wonder if, like me, they stay quiet blaming themselves instead of the guilty person? I wonder if they ever report it? Lord knows, I pray so.

I wonder about abortion, too, which was never mentioned in Papa and Mama's house. If it had been, and was safe and legal, I wonder if Mama and Papa would have given me that option? I wonder if I would have taken it?

I push the memories out of my thoughts and suddenly feel free and alive, almost euphoric. That awful frightening burden I've insisted on carrying around for all these years has finally been lifted. I shake my head and wonder why in the world I waited so long?

I take Dr. Booker's lists from the back of Malcolm's baby book and mumble the words out loud knowing that image, that everlasting image of me and Charlie, will pop into my head like it always does. Not this time I decide, not this time. I stop it before it even begins.

I tear the faded papers into teeny tiny pieces, put them in one of Mama's worn elegant ashtrays, light a match and watch them burn. I breathe a sigh of relief, pick up the phone and call Francesca.

My telling is finished.

ETTA

48

Francesca insists on taking me to lunch. We go to some fancy new restaurant on Main Street that everybody's been jabbering about. It is nice and kind of pricey for our little town, which doesn't seem to be a problem for Francesca. She's choosing appetizers, entrees, desserts, even a bottle of expensive wine.

"I'll never be able to eat all of that, child," I say, listening to her rattling off our orders to the waiter.

"What you don't eat, you can take home, Auntie.

"They give doggie bags here?"

Francesca laughs. "I don't know about that, but what we pay for we can take with us."

"All right then."

I have to admit, the food is delicious and I eat more than I intend. I even have a little wine, which is probably good too, but not to me. I'm not a wine drinker.

"This is very nice, Francesca."

"I'm glad you're enjoying it, but it seems like such a small thanks."

"For what child?"

"For agreeing to share your past and being honest with your words, for being you."

I chuckle. "If I remember correctly, you were the one who said we couldn't change our history, make it pretty or leave out what wasn't. I need to be thanking you. How did you know I had something to tell?"

She takes a sip of wine and shifts in her chair. "I always suspected Charlie was Malcolm's father."

"What made you suspicious?"

"He looked like him, Auntie."

"Not as a little boy, just when he was almost grown becoming a man."

"I only knew him when he was grown."

"Yeah, he was sure enough a man by then."

"He always reminded me of someone and seemed slightly familiar, but I could never put my finger on who."

"How did you come up with Charlie?"

"I was looking thru some of your mother's old photo albums. There was a picture of Charlie as a young man. It was like looking at Malcolm. I wondered if anybody else noticed, even knew, but I was afraid to ask. It wasn't my business and I wasn't family."

"Since when did that stop you?" I grumble.

Francesca ignores me, knows I'm kidding.

"Go on."

"You know I've always been interested in family histories."

I nod.

"I started thinking about yours. Your mother was aging. I kept thinking when she dies . . . sorry."

"Everybody dies, child."

"I didn't mean for it to sound so . . .

"It's okay, Francesca."

"I didn't want that history to be lost," she says. "Your mama agreed. I started keeping records of her words."

"I remember."

"Like you, she wasn't comfortable using the tape."

I chuckle, again.

Francesca laughs, too. "So we just talked with the machine running," she continues, dabbing at her lips. "I asked about you and Charlie and Malcolm and told her what I suspected. I knew it was a no-no. I never heard anybody talk about it. It was one of those secrets that all of you managed to keep hidden under the rug. But I figured this was my one chance at getting the truth. So I asked. You know your Mama never lied. She was honest. I never said anything to you. I didn't want to betray her confidences, but it explained a lot. I wanted to know your story but didn't want to invade your privacy either."

"Well, you know it now, child. It's all on your tapes."

"Did Charlie ever acknowledge Malcolm as his son?"

I shake my head. "No never."

"Do you think he knew?"

"He knew."

"I wonder how Malcolm would have responded?"

I swallow the last little drop of my wine and put my hand over the top of the glass so she doesn't add anymore. I've had more than enough. "Malcolm wasn't a violent man, Francesca. He was gentle and loving but I thought knowing who his daddy really was might destroy him. I couldn't have lived with that."

"Is that why you never told him?"

I nod and struggle to hide my tears. "That and . . . I suspected he knew, too."

"How?"

"I don't know how, but he knew. Like you said, as a man, he favored Charlie, but then Charlie was his uncle so that could have been seen just as a family likeness."

"And Charlie never came home?"

"Only once. After Papa died."

"That must have been something."

"It's on the tapes," I say and she doesn't pursue it.

"I can't believe Malcolm never asked or brought it up."

"Well, he didn't."

"I wonder why?"

194

"Things were different back then, child. Young folks didn't question adult matters. Besides, Malcolm was smart. He figured out I was ashamed, always ashamed that he didn't have a daddy in his life."

"He had your papa."

"Yes, he sure enough had Papa, but not a proper daddy. I felt bad about that. Still do."

"You were only fifteen, Auntie, and Charlie took advantage."

"I know, but somehow I should have known better."

"You were so attractive," she says, softly, staring at me, "was there ever a man in your life?"

"Don't think cause you treatin me like I'm special, I'm going to spill all my secrets."

"Sorry."

"I'm just pulling your leg, Francesca, I have no more secrets." I smile, push away my plate and fiddle with my wine glass. "To answer your question, Charlie kind of ruined men for me."

"How sad," she says.

"As true as that is, there were still a few." I sigh, remembering. "Only one was almost serious, but you won't find that on your tapes."

"Why?"

"Cause he wasn't a part of that story."

"How could you not hate Charlie?"

"I did, at least I tried, but hate changes nothing, child, just wears you out."

Francesca finishes the last of the wine and asks for the bill.

"You sure you can still drive?"

"I'm fine, Auntie. I'll get you home safe."

I chuckle. "I ain't worried about that. What are you going to do with the tapes?'

"After I'm finished listening, I'll copy them to disks, send one to you and put one in your family files, if that's agreeable."

195

"Send one to Becca too."

"How is she?"

"Becca's hanging in there. She has her good days and her bad."

"You want to stop by, we're close?"

"No, I never visit without calling first. You don't want to catch her on a bad day."

"Its amazing, everybody's dead now except you and Ms. Rebecca."

"Yeah, Mama lived a long life. So did Charlie." I sigh. "Malcolm . . . Malcolm got cancer, died in his fifties."

"Malcolm was a nice man," she says, "funny, always teasing."

"He did like to tease." I dab at my tears.

"You okay, Auntie?"

"I'm fine. Malcolm was a good son. I miss Malcolm."

"Did Ms. Rebecca ever forgive you?"

"Not really, we were never like sisters should be but when I got pregnant .... I shake my head. "We're civil to each other but she still blames me."

"After all these years? That's incredible, such a waste of energy."

"Don't you know I know that? But, Becca was never the forgiving type."

"Neither are you."

"What do you mean, child?"

"You've never forgiven you either."

"I'm still working on that."

These days, I often think about Becca, smart, sarcastic Becca. She was also a victim. Me getting pregnant at fifteen altered her life, too, not just the anger, but the lack of Mama's attention, of no longer being the apple of Papa's eye, no longer having a big brother and no longer growing up in a normal, close-knit loving family. She never married or had children either. I thought she was too hard on the men who courted her, too picky, was looking for the perfect mate. I now think that was just an excuse she used to hide her fear of men, though she'd never admit that. See, Charlie not only ruined men for me, he ruined men for her too. She'd never admit that either. But the truth is, Charlie ruined all our lives. I can't count the number of times I prayed I could change it, put it all back like it was before. I still do.

And even though she knows it was Charlie's fault, I try to be more understanding with Becca. I visit her daily regardless of her state of mind. I've accepted the fact she'll never forgive me. Both of us are running out of time.

Like Francesca says, I need to forgive me, too. And like I told her, I'm still working on that.

Geri Spencer Hunter is a native Iowan and a graduate of The University of Iowa College of Nursing (BSN, RN, PHN) Her writings have been published in numerous anthologies and her debut novel, *Polkadots*, was published in 1998. She is a wife, mother, grandmother and great grandmother. A retired Public Health Nurse, she lives in Sacramento, California with her husband, 'Hunter', a retired Mechanical Engineer.